Roo...

The view from the Penny... ...r
Lady Eleanor Danbury, it was the last thing she ever saw... ...ow
Cecily must find out who sent the snobbish society matron
falling to her death . . .

Do Not Disturb

Mr. Bickley answered the door knocker and ended up dead.
Cecily must capture the culprit—before murder darkens another doorstep . . .

Service for Two

Dr. McDuff's funeral became a fiasco when the mourners
found a stranger's body in the casket. Now Cecily must close
the case—for at the Pennyfoot, murder is a most unwelcome
guest . . .

Eat, Drink, and Be Buried

April showers bring May flowers—when one of the guests is
found strangled with a maypole ribbon. Soon the May Day
celebration turns into a hotel investigation—and Cecily fears
it's a merry month . . . for murder.

Check-Out Time

Life at the Pennyfoot hangs in the balance one sweltering
summer when a distinguished guest plunges to his death from
his top-floor balcony. Was it the heat . . . or cold-blooded
murder?

Grounds for Murder

The Pennyfoot's staff was put on edge when a young gypsy was
hacked to death in the woods near Badgers End. And now it's
up to Cecily to find out who at the Pennyfoot has a deadly axe
to grind . . .

Pay the Piper

The Pennyfoot's bagpipe contest ended on a sour note when
one of the pipers was murdered. Cecily must catch the killer—
before another piper pays for his visit with his life . . .

Chivalry is Dead

The jousting competition had everyone excited, until someone
began early by practicing on—and murdering—Cecily's foot-
man. Now she must discover who threw the lethal lance . . .

MORE MYSTERIES FROM THE
BERKLEY PUBLISHING GROUP . . .

SISTER FREVISSE MYSTERIES: Medieval mystery in the tradition of
Ellis Peters . . .

by Margaret Frazer

THE NOVICE'S TALE

THE OUTLAW'S TALE

THE SERVANT'S TALE

THE BISHOP'S TALE

THE BOY'S TALE

THE MURDERER'S TALE

PENNYFOOT HOTEL MYSTERIES: In Edwardian England, death
takes a seaside holiday . . .

by Kate Kingsbury

ROOM WITH A CLUE

SERVICE FOR TWO

CHECK-OUT TIME

DO NOT DISTURB

EAT, DRINK, AND BE BURIED

GROUNDS FOR MURDER

PAY THE PIPER

CHIVALRY IS DEAD

RING FOR TOMB SERVICE

GLYNIS TRYON MYSTERIES: The highly acclaimed series set in the
early days of the women's rights movement . . . "Historically accurate
and telling." —Sara Paretsky

by Miriam Grace Monfredo

SENECA FALLS INHERITANCE

BLACKWATER SPIRITS

NORTH STAR CONSPIRACY

THROUGH A GOLD EAGLE

MARK TWAIN MYSTERIES: "Adventurous . . . Replete with genuine tall tales from the great man himself." —*Mostly Murder*

by Peter J. Heck

DEATH ON THE MISSISSIPPI

A CONNECTICUT YANKEE IN CRIMINAL COURT

CHAPTER

1

Phoebe Carter-Holmes's delicate face looked quite pained as she sat herself down at the long polished table in the library of the Pennyfoot Hotel. "I really don't know where on earth I am going to find one hundred people to dance around the church," she exclaimed. "Sometimes I do believe that Algie takes unfair advantage of me. There are definite drawbacks to being the mother of a vicar."

The willowy woman seated opposite her uttered a low, mocking laugh. "Nonsense, Phoebe. You know you adore bossing people around. Nothing makes you happier."

Phoebe directed a disdainful glance at Madeline Pengrath. "At least I achieve something worthwhile with my efforts. I don't have to resort to hocus-pocus to impress people."

1

Madeline smiled. "It's such a pity you don't believe in the powers of herbal medicines. I have the perfect remedy for Algie's unfortunate stutter."

Phoebe tossed her head with such force that a wisp of mauve feather detached itself from the large plume decorating her enormous hat. It floated gently down and rested comfortably on her nose.

With a small sound of irritation, Phoebe wafted it away with a flick of her gloved fingers and turned to the third member of the group seated at the head of the Jacobean table.

"Cecily, dear, do you suppose the members of your bicycle club would consent to assist us with the clipping?"

Cecily Sinclair, the owner of the Pennyfoot Hotel, was only half aware of the conversation. Her thoughts had been concentrated on her new manager. Ever since Baxter, her last manager, had left her employ three months ago, the paperwork in the office had been mounting up at an alarming rate, to the point where she could no longer cope with it.

She had hired Malcolm Ridlington more out of desperation than anything, and now she wasn't sure that she had done the right thing. The problem was, she thought gloomily, absolutely no one could ever match up to Baxter. Professionally or personally.

"Cecily? Are you all right?"

Cecily looked up with a start to find two pairs of eyes regarding her. Madeline's dark gaze was knowing and full of sympathy. Phoebe merely looked put out.

"I have spoken to you twice already," she said, sounding a trifle offended. "I do hope and trust I'm not intruding on your thoughts?"

"I'm sorry, Phoebe," Cecily said hastily, "I must admit

my thoughts were elsewhere. Please forgive me. What was it you were saying?"

"I asked you," Phoebe repeated, speaking slowly and clearly as if Cecily were deaf, "if you thought that the members of your bicycle club would assist us with the Clipping of the Church ceremony."

Cecily blinked. "Bicycle?"

Phoebe heaved her prominent bosom in an exaggerated sigh. "You are expecting fifty members of a London bicycle club this afternoon, are you not?"

"Oh, the women's bicycle club." Cecily nodded. "Yes, of course. I'm sorry, Phoebe, I seem to be just a little preoccupied."

Phoebe sniffed. "Perhaps you should make an appointment to see Dr. Prestwick. In my opinion, you have not been yourself for quite some time."

"Ever since the estimable Baxter left, in fact," Madeline said wickedly.

Cecily shot her a warning glance before turning to the other woman. "Please don't concern yourself, Phoebe. I am in good health. It is just that with all the office work falling behind, I'm a little concerned as to how my new manager is getting along."

"Well, we all know he won't be another Baxter," Madeline said, ignoring Cecily's scowl. "So don't expect too much from poor Mr. Ridlington."

"Thank you, Madeline. I'll bear that in mind. Now, what is it you wish to ask the club members, Phoebe?"

"I have to find at least a hundred people for the clipping. I thought they might like to help out."

Cecily gave her a blank look. "You want them to help you clip the hedges?"

Madeline chuckled as Phoebe's cheeks turned pink.

"No, Cecily dear," Phoebe said carefully. "I thought I

explained that Algie wants to arrange the Clipping of the Church ceremony in honor of the bishop's visit to Badgers End. After all, St. Bartholomew's Week is a celebration to commemorate the birthday of our church's saint. It is only fitting that we do something special involving the church."

Cecily's brow cleared as her memory supplied the answer to the mystery. "Oh, now I remember. That's the ceremony where everyone joins hands and encircles the church."

"Quite." Phoebe sat back with a look of relief on her face. "When the circle is complete, everyone sings and dances, thus clipping the church, or embracing it, if you will. Algie thinks the ceremony will be a fitting finale to the week's celebrations. That's why he wants to do it on Friday, seeing as the garden fete and flower show will be on the Saturday."

"I think that's a very good idea," Cecily murmured.

Phoebe sat forward again with a look of alarm. "You haven't forgotten that the bishop will be arriving this afternoon for the feast of St. Bartholomew?"

Cecily shook her head. "No, Phoebe, I can hardly forget that event, considering that the feast will be held here at the hotel tonight."

Phoebe looked relieved. "He will be bringing us the Helmsboro chalice this afternoon, of course. It will be on display during St. Bartholomew's Week." She clasped her hands and cast her eyes toward the ceiling. "I can hardly wait to see the chalice. It is on loan from the Abbey for such a short while, and only a few churches have been selected to place the cup on display."

Madeline snorted. "All this fuss over a silly cup. It isn't even gold from what I hear."

Phoebe stiffened her back, stretching her chin above the lace ruffle at her throat. "For your information, Madeline, the chalice was fashioned for King Charles II. It happens to be made of pewter and is encrusted with pure gold and jewels."

"How terribly bourgeois."

"The chalice," Phoebe said coldly, "is usually reserved for only the most influential confirmations, but someone thought it would be nice if ordinary people could have a glimpse of the cup." She leaned forward slightly. "But then, of course, there are always those who are too ignorant to appreciate something of such priceless value."

"The chalice sounds wonderful, Phoebe," Cecily said, giving Madeline a beseeching look. "I'm looking forward to seeing it myself."

Phoebe turned eagerly to her more appreciative audience. "It is such an honor to be singled out this way. Algie can't imagine why St. Bartholomew's was chosen to display the chalice. After all, we are such a small, insignificant parish, but, as I told Algie, news of his dedication to the church and his wonderful, inspiring sermons must have reached the bishop's ears."

"More likely the bishop heard about all that yawning and snoring that Algie's sermons inspire and decided to liven things up a bit," Madeline said dryly.

Phoebe visibly bristled. "I do not have to sit here and listen to insulting comments from someone who knows nothing about religious artifacts."

"How can you say that, Phoebe dear, when I'm looking right at one?"

"Madeline, please?" Cecily held out her hands in appeal.

"Oh, very well." Madeline rose, tossing her long dark hair over her shoulders with a majestic sweep of her hand. "I have to be going, in any case. I have to arrange the flowers for the feast, and I still have to take care of the final arrangements for the flower show on Saturday."

"Perhaps that will keep you out of our hair for a while," Phoebe said with a disdainful glance at her tormentor.

"Out of Cecily's hair, at least." Madeline floated across the room and paused at the door. "I will see you on Saturday, then, Cecily?"

Cecily nodded, relieved to see her friend go. Much as she loved Madeline, the constant bickering between her and Phoebe could be intolerable at times.

Glancing at Phoebe, Cecily could tell from the red spots high on the other woman's cheeks that Madeline's parting shot had found its mark. Although no one knew for sure, it was generally suspected among the staff of the Pennyfoot that Phoebe's hair was actually a wig. The fact that no one had ever seen her without one of her enormous hats added fuel to the rumor.

Feeling sorry for the woman, Cecily leaned forward and patted her hand. "Don't take Madeline's words to heart, Phoebe. She does genuinely care for you. Madeline has trouble dealing with emotions. It's her way of paying you attention."

"Really. Well, that kind of attention I can well do without, thank you."

Cecily decided it was time to change the subject. "Tell me, Phoebe, how is Algie dealing with all the excitement of the bishop's visit?"

Phoebe produced a lace-edged handkerchief from her sleeve and waved it in front of her face. The fragrance of lavender water wafted across the table. "Oh, you know Algie. Twittering with nerves and worrying himself silly that he'll do something wrong and disgrace himself. He has no confidence in himself whatsoever. I have no idea who he takes after. Certainly not dear departed Sedgely, nor myself for that matter."

"I'm quite sure he'll manage beautifully," Cecily murmured, glancing at the clock on the mantelpiece. She needed to be in the office in case her new manager needed her assistance. She would have put an end to the meeting, except that Phoebe seemed inclined to chatter on.

"It is so nice the bishop was able to have a suite here at the hotel. I just know that Algie would have had a pink fit if we had been forced to put him up at the vicarage."

"I'm glad he booked early; otherwise we might not have had a room," Cecily said, gathering up her notebook in the hopes that Phoebe would take the hint.

"Quite so, this being the middle of August. The bicycle club must be the biggest group you've had at the Pennyfoot, is it not? How did you arrange that?"

"I didn't." Cecily sent a meaningful glance at the clock. "Apparently a London banker recommended us. The bank is sponsoring the event."

"Well, I sincerely hope that your more elite clientele don't take offense at being ousted by a group of women riding bicycles. I can't imagine what the world is coming to, when women can gallivant unescorted across the country astride an abominable machine."

"I understand most of the women will be bringing their husbands," Cecily said mildly. "As for our regular clients, most of them don't care to come down to Badgers End during St. Bartholomew's Week. It's too crowded. As you know, the aristocracy prefer their privacy."

"Only because they are ashamed to let their acquaintances know what they are up to," Phoebe retorted. "No doubt some of the goings-on in this hotel would make your teeth curl if you did but know it."

"No doubt." Cecily pushed back her chair and rose. "I'm sorry, Phoebe, but I really have to look in on my new manager now."

"Oh, yes, of course." Phoebe got fussily to her feet,

smoothing, tugging and straightening her immaculate oyster silk two-piece frock. "I just hope you have made a more fortunate choice than you did with your new doorman. A very strange fellow, if you ask me. I can't understand him at all. He appears to be talking English, but it sounds like a foreign language."

"Cockney slang, Phoebe. Surely even you must have heard of it?"

Phoebe reached for her mauve parasol and shook it to smooth out the folds. Smoothing her fingers up her elbow-length glove, she murmured, "Oh, yes, I do believe I have. It's that dreadful way the East End Londoners have of talking. Never could understand it, of course, which is why they do it, I suppose. Though what on earth those commoners think they have to hide that could possibly interest us, I have no idea."

"Well, I'm sure Ned has nothing to hide. He seems to be a very nice young man."

Phoebe swept to the door, paused, then turned back to give Cecily a sly look. "It's none of my business, of course, but don't you think you might be lowering the tone of the place by hiring such a vulgar person for your doorman? I'm quite sure were Baxter here he would never have consented to such a . . . strange choice."

"You are quite right, Phoebe; it is none of your business." Cecily softened the words with a smile. "I'll look forward to seeing you at the ceremony on Friday."

Phoebe looked affronted, then shook her head and sailed out of the door, closing it behind her with a little more force than usual.

Cecily winced. Perhaps she had been a little short. It was never pleasant to have one's doubts confirmed. She had hired Ned Harris on the spur of the moment, mainly because he was the only person who applied for the job in three weeks. He seemed to be a cheerful young man, fairly intelligent, and smartly, if somewhat flashily, dressed.

His unfortunate speech pattern, a strange form of rhyming slang commonly used by the London cockneys, was confusing, but Ned had promised to speak "proper" when addressing the guests. The fact that his references were vague and impossible to follow up had seemed a minor point when faced with desperation. In fact, Malcolm Ridlington's references had not been much better.

Glancing up at the portrait of her late husband that hung over the marble fireplace, Cecily grimaced. At one time she had found solace in talking to James's portrait. After his unfortunate death from malaria several years earlier, somehow she had felt closer to him when she was able to tell his image about her worries.

Now, looking at the erect, smiling figure in his military uniform, he no longer seemed the compassionate, comforting presence he once had been. Now he was just a painting of someone she had known and loved, but whom she no longer held in her heart.

Another man held that place now. A man who cared so little for her he had deserted her and the Pennyfoot, without a word as to where he was going. Nor had he sent word to her since. To all intents and purposes, Baxter had walked out of her life, without any intention of ever coming back.

If she had any sense, Cecily told herself as she made her way to the office, she would forget that Baxter had ever existed. But then, when did a woman in love ever have any sense?

Shocked that she had finally admitted the truth about her feelings, Cecily paused for a moment before tapping on the door of the office.

This was the moment she had always enjoyed, the anticipation of spending a few minutes alone with Baxter.

Now there was only a feeling of emptiness and an ache that wouldn't go away. Now she knew why. Shaken by the thought, she made an effort to pull herself together.

Her summons on the door was answered immediately by a curt "Come in!"

Malcolm Ridlington sat at the desk, a pen clenched in his thick fingers. His bushy, dark brows were drawn together above his hawkish nose, which supported a pair of flimsy glasses. In front of him a sheaf of papers had been scattered across the desk, as if swept there by an irritated hand.

Upon seeing her, the manager rose awkwardly to his feet. A sheen of perspiration glistened on his forehead, no doubt because of the heavy black morning coat he still wore.

Cecily tried not to remember how Baxter always scrambled into his coat whenever she entered the office unannounced.

"Mrs. Sinclair," Malcolm said in his low, quiet voice. "Is there something I can do for you?"

The longing for a cigar almost overwhelmed her. It was on the tip of her tongue to ask her new manager if he smoked them, but then she thought better of it. "I just wanted to see how you are coping with the accounts. I'm afraid things have got a little out of hand since Baxter left."

"So I can see." Malcolm glanced across the desk. "It has taken me all morning just to separate the debits from the credits."

"I'm sorry." Cecily averted her gaze from the door to Baxter's old room. It was Malcolm's room now. She had to remember that. "I was wondering if you planned to join us for the feast tonight," she said brightly. "Perhaps you would care to share my table. Then we can discuss any problems that may have arisen."

"Thank you, madam, but I will not have time to indulge in leisurely pursuits. I have too much work to do sorting out this ghastly mess that your last manager left behind."

Cecily opened her mouth to protest, then closed it again. Nothing would be gained by arguing with him. She turned to leave, feeling guilty for not leaping to Baxter's defense. After all, she was the one who had allowed the paperwork to fall into such disorder.

Trudging up the hallway, she sadly reflected that the state of the hotel accounts was not the only casualty of Baxter's departure. Somehow she could no longer generate an interest in resolving the problems of the hotel. If she didn't pull herself together, she could very well lose the Pennyfoot. If that happened, she had no doubt in her mind that James Sinclair would come back to haunt her.

CHAPTER

2

"He's here, Algie, so please stop twittering and fasten that top button on your cassock." Phoebe cast a critical eye over her son's portly figure in the long, black robe, then, mildly satisfied, turned to bestow her brightest smile at the bishop, whose feet crunched loudly on the gravel as he approached the church door.

"Reverend Hornsworth!" she trilled as the stout figure paused at the steps. "How absolutely wonderful to see you again."

The bishop frowned. "We have met, madam?"

"Yes, Bishop, yes, indeed. It was when my son, Algernon Carter-Holmes, was ordained." Groping behind her, Phoebe grasped the sleeve of Algie's cassock and tugged. "I'm sure you remember the vicar of Badgers End?"

13

"Oh, quite, quite." The bishop peered shortsightedly at Algie, who stood quivering so violently that Phoebe could see the hem of his cassock vibrating like a plucked viola string.

"Speak," she muttered through gritted teeth.

"Ah . . . so nice to s-s-see you . . . ah . . . again, B-b-b-b—"

Phoebe dug her elbow smartly into Algie's side.

He gave a little gasp then managed, "B-bishop."

Hornsworth stared at Algie as if he'd grown two heads. "Quite," he murmured, sending a hunted look over his shoulder at the trap, which waited for him at the curb.

"Did you bring it with you?" Phoebe asked anxiously.

"Bring it?" The bishop's pale blue eyes looked apprehensive.

"The chalice." She peered down the path as if expecting the cup to come walking along by itself.

"Oh, yes, of course. The chalice. That's why I'm here."

Algie gave a little squeak of relief.

Phoebe sent him a scathing glance, then turned back to the bishop. "Can the vicar carry it in for you?"

Hornsworth sent a horrified glance in Algie's direction. "Oh, no, thank you. It's very heavy, you see. I left it in the trap. I'll just go and fetch it, shall I?" He turned smartly on his heel and hurried back to the trap, his cassock flapping around his ankles.

Phoebe sighed. "How many times do I have to tell you, Algie? Take a deep breath before you speak. No one is going to understand you when you stutter like that."

Algie gasped and drew in a gulp of air. "I can't help it," he muttered. "After all, it isn't . . . ah . . . every day we have a b-bishop visit St. Bartholomew's."

"Thank the heavens for that," Phoebe said tartly, "or you would be lashing yourself to death with your tongue."

"There's no need to be uncivil." Algie tossed his head and made a grab at his glasses, which had slid down his nose.

"Shush!" Phoebe put a gloved finger delicately against her lips. "He's coming back."

John Hornsworth staggered up the path with a large glass case in his arms. Phoebe felt an intense excitement at the mere sight of the case. The contents, as yet, were hidden by the sleeves of the bishop's cassock.

"Do be careful," she warned as he ducked his head to step inside the church. "I should hate for something to happen to such a valuable relic."

The bishop merely grunted. His face had turned a bright red, and sweat stood out on his brow as he struggled toward the pedestal.

"Help him, Algie," Phoebe ordered as the other man reached the pedestal and stood there looking as if he wasn't sure where to put down the case.

"I assume this is where you intend to display it?" he asked breathlessly.

Phoebe gave Algie a sharp push. The vicar stumbled forward, muttering and bumbling unintelligible words. He did, however, manage to assist Hornsworth in raising the glass case to the pedestal and setting it firmly in place.

Phoebe gave a little gasp as the two men stepped back to review their handiwork. The huge chalice sat on a red velvet cushion in the center of the case. Sunlight, slanting through the stained-glass window behind it, seemed to set the cup alight. Fiery rubies flashed in their bed of gleaming gold, overpowering the cool splendor of magnificent emeralds.

"It is breathtaking," Phoebe whispered, certain she had never seen anything so beautiful in all her born days.

"It is, indeed," the bishop agreed, nodding and smiling as he surveyed the treasure. "I happen to be an avid collector of religious artifacts. This piece, however, far outshines anything in my collection. It is priceless, of course, which is why I must chain it to the pedestal."

Phoebe watched as he reached up and unwound a length of thick chain from around the base of the case. Stooping, he passed the chain twice around the foot of the pedestal, then locked it with a small padlock.

"That should do it," he muttered, and straightened.

Phoebe glanced at Algie, who stood with his hands clasped together, his face glowing with pride as if he had fashioned the cup himself.

"It must be very heavy," Phoebe remarked, turning back to the bishop.

"It is, madam. Extremely so. Of course, the case weighs quite a bit as well, but I can assure you it takes two strong hands to lift that chalice to the lips of a fledgling member of our church."

"I am quite sure you have no trouble at all, Bishop," Phoebe murmured coyly.

Hornsworth glanced at her, then cleared his throat. "Yes, well, that's as may be. I had better be going. I have to book into the hotel."

"Ah, yes. My dear friend, Cecily Sinclair, is expecting you. She's the owner, you know." Phoebe tripped along behind the hurrying figure of the bishop, leaving Algie still staring speechlessly at his treasure.

"Yes, yes. Quite, quite." Hornsworth reached the door and turned back for one last look at the chalice. "I'm sure it will be safe there," he murmured as if to reassure himself.

"Quite safe, Bishop. Have no fear. Algie will guard it with his life."

The bishop looked as if that was his biggest worry.

"Of course," Phoebe hastened to assure him, "the pedestal is embedded in solid concrete, and your chain looks very secure."

"It is," Hornsworth said, turning slowly back to the door. "The strongest steel imaginable."

"Shall we see you at the feast tonight?" Phoebe asked hopefully. "Both Algie and I are invited, you know. I am sure Algie would be delighted if you would join us at our table."

"I'm not aware of the arrangements for dining as yet," Hornsworth muttered. "I do thank you for the invitation, though."

"Oh, entirely my pleasure, Bishop." Phoebe fluttered her eyelashes, but the bishop was already heading down the path, waving his hand in a brief farewell.

"Such a nice man," she gushed as she came back to join Algie at the pedestal.

Algie nodded, then turned with a start as a quavery voice spoke from the vestry door. "Begging your pardon, mum, but can I have a look at it?"

Phoebe beckoned with an imperious finger at the frail man who stood in the doorway. "Come in, Will, and feast your eyes on this magnificent sight."

Will Jones shuffled toward the pedestal, his back bent over with advancing age. He stood next to Algie, who finally regained his speech.

"Marvelous, isn't it?" Algie said in a hushed voice. "I can't believe our little church was . . . ah . . . chosen for such an honor."

"Bloody beautiful, that," Will said with due reverence.

"The bishop looked very well, I thought," Phoebe murmured. "I am surprised he didn't recognize me at first, though. Mind you, he has lost a little weight since I saw him last. Or perhaps he just seems taller than what I remember. What do you think, Algie?"

Algie appeared not to hear her. He was lost once more in

his adoration for the chalice. For once, Phoebe let him muse in peace.

The Pennyfoot's roof garden, created by James during the hotel's renovation from the country home of an earl, remained a haven to Cecily long after James had died. Nowadays she rarely visited the flower-bedecked area between the sloping roofs, largely because she hadn't the time.

That evening, however, she escaped for a few brief moments of respite from the frantic preparations for the feast. Dressed in her favorite periwinkle blue gown, she took a few deep breaths of cool, clean air as she gazed across the calm bay to the far horizon.

She used to ache with loneliness for James whenever she stood here, watching the fishing boats bob in the harbor. Now it was Baxter she longed to see.

The sound of the attic door closing softly behind her turned her head. For a moment she thought she was dreaming, the vision conjured up by her poignant thoughts. But then the figure moved away from the shadows.

"Hello, Cecily," Baxter said quietly.

Her breath seemed captured in her throat, and her fingers fluttered there as she stared at his tall, imposing figure. He looked much the same, elegant as always in a black evening suit and crisp white shirt, his bow tie meticulously fastened.

The dying sunlight gleamed in the silver streaks at his temples, and as she gazed on his beloved face, she knew there was a difference after all. It was in his eyes.

Her heart skittered crazily, and she took a moment to regain her breath. "Baxter," she said with just the right amount of pleased surprise. "I had no idea you were in town."

"I wanted to surprise you. My firm has closed for the

week for the annual holidays, so I decided to come down and pay you a visit."

She should be angry with him, she thought. This was the first she'd heard from him since he left. Looking upon his face once more, she knew she could not waste these moments in anger. "You work in London now, I take it?"

He gave her a brief nod. "It's good to see you again, Cecily."

It seemed strange, and quite wonderful, to hear him address her by her Christian name. He had used it so rarely in the past. "And you, too, Baxter." She gave a little gasp. "Oh, dear, I do wish you had let me know you were coming. The hotel is full this week. We have fifty members of a bicycle club staying here."

"Please, don't concern yourself. I have booked in at the George and Dragon. I shall be quite comfortable there."

She tried not to reveal her dismay at this news. Hurt at the thought he preferred the inn to the Pennyfoot, she merely shrugged. "Perhaps it is just as well," she murmured, without really knowing what she meant. "You will stay for the feast tonight, though, will you not?"

Baxter inclined his head. "I would be delighted. The St. Bartholomew's feast has always been one of my favorite meals. I trust Michel is still creating his wonderful soufflés?"

She smiled. "He is. Nothing much has changed, except . . ." She paused, while Baxter looked at her, his eyebrow raised in the quizzical expression she knew so well. "I have a new manager," she finished flatly.

"Ah. I thought you might." He regarded her solemnly. "I trust he is working out well?"

"Quite well, thank you." She dropped her gaze, flustered for some reason by his intent scrutiny. "We should be getting along to the dining room, I suppose."

He moved to the door and held it open for her. "After you, dear madam."

She passed through, wondering if she had heard aright. Intensely aware of him behind her, she descended the stairs, chattering about the hotel in order to cover her confusion.

"We have a new doorman, as well," she said as they turned the corner on the first landing. "Ned Harris. He's from London, too. Perhaps you saw him when you arrived?"

"I saw him," Baxter said, sounding unimpressed.

Reaching the main hallway, Cecily breathed a sigh of relief. Her knees had felt somewhat unsteady all the way down. As Baxter joined her at the base of the stairs, a tall, stocky woman wearing a dull pink tea gown approached them.

"Good evening, Mrs. Sinclair," the woman said in a booming voice.

"Miss Parsons. Have you met my manag—my ex-manager, Mr. Baxter?"

Cecily watched as Baxter gave the woman a polite bow. "So pleased to make your acquaintance, madam," he murmured.

The woman swept a glance at him and barely nodded. "Likewise, I'm sure. Mrs. Sinclair, I shall not be attending the feast tonight. I have a weak stomach, you know. I'm not feeling well after that long ride. I think I prefer to have a light meal in my room tonight."

"Certainly, Miss Parsons. I'll see that it's brought up to you."

The woman gathered up her skirt, muttering, "Goodnight to you, Mrs. Sinclair, Mr. Baxter," then clumsily mounted the stairs.

"That woman doesn't look as if anything about her is weak," Baxter commented as he accompanied Cecily down the hallway toward the dining room.

Soft music from a string orchestra drifted toward them as Cecily looked up at him in surprise. It wasn't like Baxter to pass comments on the guests. In fact, he often chastised her for doing so.

"That was the president of the woman's bicycle club, Miss Primrose Parsons," she said with a faint note of reproof.

"Anyone less like a flower I have never seen." He lowered his voice to a conspiratorial whisper. "In fact," he said, "had she not obviously been endowed with a bosom, I should suspect her of being a man."

Stunned by this irreverence from someone who was always so intensely proper, Cecily took several moments to answer him. In fact, they had been seated at her table in the corner of the dining room before she regained her composure enough to order a tray for Miss Parsons.

Left alone with Baxter, she managed to say lightly, "I must say that life in the big city seems to have had rather a strange effect on you."

He smiled at her, and she was discomfited further when she saw a gleam in his eye. "Does it, indeed?" he murmured.

Hastily changing the subject, Cecily began talking about the bicycle club members, all of whom had arrived safely that afternoon. "They are quite an interesting group of people," she said, looking around at the crowded tables. "Though I fear we might have a problem with one or two of them."

"In what way?" Baxter asked, looking as if he'd rather talk about something else.

Strangely afraid to discover what he preferred to discuss, Cecily said doggedly, "There's one young man, Sid Barker. I overheard him arguing quite strenuously with Ned, the doorman. It was difficult to know what about, since Ned has

an unfortunate habit of using cockney slang, but it was
heated enough for me to have to intervene."

"Perhaps it is your doorman who caused the argument,"
Baxter suggested.

"That is a possibility, of course." Cecily frowned. "But
then, a little later on, I heard another heated exchange
between Mr. Barker and Miss Parsons. Apparently she was
questioning his eligibility to be a member. Mr. Barker was
quite adamant about it. I do hope he is not going to be a
disruptive element this week."

"Is he here now?" Baxter asked, turning his head to
survey the room.

Cecily also studied the tables. "He's a strange young man,
quite effeminate really. He has such delicate features, and
his hair falls all over his face. Not at all the type you'd think
would be interested in a sport as strenuous as long-distance
bicycle riding."

She craned her neck to see across the room. "He doesn't
appear to be here tonight, however. I wonder if he also has
a weak stomach."

"What about your new manager?" Baxter asked casually.
"Is he here?"

Cecily shook her head. "Malcolm expected to work late
this evening. I'm afraid I let things get rather in a mess since
you left."

Baxter smiled. "You missed me?"

"Yes," she said, feeling again that strange flutter in her
breast. "We all do. I don't know if Malcolm Ridlington is
the right choice. He was a financial consultant for a Scottish
countess. Apparently she died, leaving Malcolm without a
job. He seems to have a grasp of the business, and certainly
seems intelligent enough. He's just . . ."

"Yes?" Baxter prompted.

"He's just not you," she said simply.

"Ah," Baxter said with such depth she was left wondering exactly what he'd meant by that simple word. "And what about Dr. Prestwick?" he added before she could comment. "I can't see his beguiling face here tonight."

His sarcasm was not lost on Cecily, but she preferred to ignore it. "He was invited," she said demurely. "He must have had a previous engagement."

"For which I'm eternally grateful."

Cecily was well aware of Baxter's dislike of the charismatic doctor, though she was never fully certain as to the reason. She rather hoped it had something to do with Baxter's regard for her, but this didn't seem the time to question him about that.

The evening passed swiftly, with every sign that the guests were thoroughly enjoying the magnificent meal that Michel had prepared. Trays of lobster, partridge, and grouse and huge barons of beef were quickly demolished by the chattering, laughing revelers, with the bishop's hearty belly laugh overpowering the entire room.

Several times Cecily's conversation with Baxter was punctuated by the irritating sound, until Baxter remarked sourly, "If that gentleman were not a man of God, I would say the devil had sent him to annoy us all."

Studying his familiar face, Cecily felt a pang of uneasiness. There was no doubt that Baxter had changed, though she wasn't entirely sure it was for the better. He was more relaxed, more confident, and more worldly than she had ever seen him.

He had been extremely attentive all evening, unsettling her with his constant use of "dear madam." She detected a hint of some hidden purpose in his eyes that she couldn't define, and for the first time since she'd known him she felt insecure in his presence.

If she didn't know better, she thought with a flurry of

nerves, she'd think he was attempting to court her. Which was a ridiculous idea, of course. Even so, when he bowed low over her hand and pressed his lips to her fingers before taking his leave of her later, she felt as if the years were dropping away, leaving her feeling disgustingly youthful.

The feeling stayed with her throughout a restless night. The following morning, however, her odd euphoria vanished when Mrs. Chubb brought up the morning hot water herself instead of sending it up with a housemaid.

Sensing trouble, Cecily gazed with apprehension at the housekeeper's normally jovial face. As always, her first thoughts flew to her sons. News traveled so slowly from abroad. If something happened to either one of them, it would be days before she heard. Too late for her to be there for them.

"I'm sorry to disturb you, mum," Mrs. Chubb said a trifle breathlessly. "I thought you'd like to know, seeing as how Mrs. Carter-Holmes is such a good friend."

Cecily clutched her throat in alarm. "Phoebe? Something's happened to Phoebe?"

Mrs. Chubb vigorously shook her head. "Oh, no, mum, she's just fine, thank the Lord. It's the bell ringer at the church, I'm afraid. Will Jones. They found his body caught in some rocks in Devil's Cauldron early this morning. According to Samuel, the police reckon he fell off the cliff on his way home last night."

"How dreadful. The poor man." Cecily watched her housekeeper pour hot water into the basin from the huge china jug. Knowing that Mrs. Chubb shared her fondness for Phoebe, she added, "I'll pay Phoebe a visit this morning. She must be quite shaken by this sad event."

"Yes, mum. I expect she is." The housekeeper swung around and hurried to the door, her keys jangling noisily from her belt. "If you'll excuse me, mum, I must get back to the kitchen. With so many guests to take care of, it's hard to keep pace with everything."

Cecily nodded, her thoughts already assessing the effects of the tragedy. It was a sober start to the celebrations of St. Bartholomew's Week. And, although she found it impossible to explain why, for some reason she had an uneasy premonition that worse was to follow.

CHAPTER

3

"I tell you, I'm at me bleeding wit's end, I am," Gertie announced, shoving a hank of black hair away from her perspiring face. "What with all this bloody extra work and the twins getting into Gawd knows what, I don't know if I'm on me blinking head or me heels."

"I'm not getting into anything, Miss Brown," Doris said meekly. She stood in the pantry doorway with a pathetic look on her face, her fingers pleating the folds of her long white apron.

Gertie eyed the slender girl with scorn. "Not you, you bleeding nitwit. I'm not talking about you and Daisy. I'm talking about me own twins, Lilly and James."

"Lillian," Mrs. Chubb corrected, without turning away

from the cast-iron stove where she stirred hot treacle in a massive enameled iron pot.

Gertie sent the pudgy housekeeper a baleful glance. "Lillian, then. Bleeding all right, ain't it, when I can't call me own daughter what I want."

"You named the child after me, and my middle name is Lillian." Mrs. Chubb gave the wide wooden spoon a final flourish and lifted it from the sticky mixture. Thin strands of golden syrup streamed back into the pot, making Gertie's mouth water.

Putting a curb on her sweet tooth, she finished polishing the brandy glass in her hand with her soft cloth. Lifting the glass up to the light, she gave it a cursory inspection before setting it down on the scrubbed wooden table. "Anyway, as I was saying when I was so bleeding rudely interrupted, I don't know what I'm going to do with those flipping babies, I'm sure I don't."

"What's the matter now, Gertie? You're always complaining lately." Mrs. Chubb whisked the spoon over to the sink before the treacle could spill on the floor. "You should be thanking your lucky stars those babies are so healthy instead of complaining about them."

"Healthy?" Gertie gave a loud snort. "I'll bleeding say they're healthy. It's me what's bloody run-down. Look at me eyes, all bleeding bloodshot an' all. I've got bags under 'em big enough to pack an eiderdown in, that's what."

"Daisy says as how the babies are beginning to stand on their own," Doris said helpfully. "Won't be long before they're walking, I reckon."

Gertie slapped a glass onto the table, making the rest of them rattle and clink. "There! See what I bleeding mean? Bloody *walking*. What am I supposed to blinking do with them then, I ask you? Daisy can't give up any more bleeding time to look after them."

"Daisy likes looking after them," Doris said, carrying a large cauldron of milk over to the stove. She struggled with it for a moment or two, trying to lift the cumbersome container with arms that looked like sticks.

"Strewth!" Gertie rolled her eyes to the ceiling and dropped her cloth on the table. "Come here and bleeding give the thing to me, then." She took the cauldron from Doris and dumped it effortlessly onto the stove.

"Thank you, Miss Brown."

Gertie frowned at the hapless maid. "Blimey, Doris, you ain't half thin. You'd better start eating your blinking porridge or you'll bleeding fade away."

"Yes, Miss Brown." Doris hitched up her skirt and fled back to the pantry.

"You're right about Daisy," Mrs. Chubb said, rinsing her hands under the tap. "With all this extra work, we need her here in the kitchen. Michel is getting very testy these days. Not that I can blame him when half the jobs aren't done when he gets here."

"If you ask me," Gertie muttered, "Michel could bleeding do some of his own dirty work. Just 'cause he's the flipping chef don't mean he's blinking royalty. What's bloody stopping him from cleaning his own brussels sprouts, that's what I want to know?"

"You know very well the chef doesn't clean vegetables."

"Well, nor do blinking head housemaids, neither. So why am I bloody doing it, then?"

"Because we're shorthanded, that's why." Mrs. Chubb pulled a bag of flour off the shelf and opened it. "What with Daisy taking care of the babies, we've all got to put a little extra effort in."

"I knew this weren't going to work," Gertie said, trying to still the flutter of panic in her stomach. "I shall have to give up me bleeding job to look after them, that's what. Then what am I flipping going to do for money?"

Mrs. Chubb sighed as she measured flour into a yellow mixing bowl. "It's just too bad that Ian went off and left you like that. Those poor little babies growing up without a father. It's a tragedy, that's what it is."

"Never mind the bleeding babies, what about me?" Gertie stacked glasses onto a huge silver tray. "I'm the one what's got to worry about blinking feeding and clothing them."

"Well, perhaps we can all keep an eye on them here in the kitchen while we're working. Give them a pot or two to play with. That will keep them occupied."

"For how bleeding long, though? And what will Michel say when he sees two flipping babies crawling all over the floor?"

Mrs. Chubb dusted her hands on her apron. "I'll handle Michel, don't you worry yourself about that. One way or another, we'll manage."

Doris emerged from the pantry, carrying a sack of potatoes. Gertie watched her struggle over to the sink and lift the sack high enough to let the potatoes tumble out. She waited for the thunderous rattle to subside before saying, "Has anyone seen the new doorman yet?"

Doris sent a nervous glance over her shoulder. "I haven't, Miss Brown, but Daisy said she spoke to him yesterday. She couldn't understand him, she said. He talks funny."

Mrs. Chubb stopped pummeling the bread dough and lifted her head. "Talks funny? Whatever do you mean?"

"She means he talks bleeding cockney," Gertie said. She pulled the dresser drawer open and lifted out the heavy tray of cutlery. "Ned Harris comes from east London. They all bleeding talk like that there. You know, rhyming slang."

"I've heard mention of it." Mrs. Chubb resumed her

kneading. "I believe they replace proper words with a word that rhymes."

"Yeah, that's right. Instead of saying stairs, they say apples and pears, and they call feet bloody plates of meat."

"Sounds ridiculous to me," Mrs. Chubb muttered.

Gertie shrugged. "Does sound bleeding daft, I s'pose, if you're not one of them. What makes it bloody hard to understand is when they don't say the whole bleeding thing. Instead of saying apples and pears, they just say apples. Then you have to work out what goes with bloody apples before you can guess what bleeding rhymes with it."

Mrs. Chubb made a clicking noise with her tongue. "How on earth is anyone supposed to understand it, then?"

"You're not supposed to blinking understand it. Not unless you're one of them."

"Well, I'm not one of them. Nor are any of our guests. I'm surprised madam hired someone like that to be a doorman. I just hope he keeps his mouth shut, or we'll be having a lot of confused people wandering around this hotel." Mrs. Chubb slapped the dough as if she wished it were Ned Harris's face.

"Oh, don't get your bleeding drawers in a twist," Gertie said, sorting through the knives on the tray. "Ned promised madam he'd talk proper when the guests are around. In any case, I offered to explain what he means if I hear him bloody talking like that."

"Really?" The housekeeper lifted her chin with a jerk. "And just how are you supposed to do that when we have all this extra work on our hands, might I ask?"

Doris dropped the potato she was peeling in the water with a splash. Nervously scrabbling for it, she rattled the rest of the potatoes around in the sink.

Gertie sighed. "I only meant if I was passing through, that's all."

"Sounds as if you and this Ned Harris had quite a conversation," Mrs. Chubb said with a note of reprimand in her voice.

Gertie grinned. "We bleeding did. Lovely, it were. He's a right bleeding smasher, that Ned. I wouldn't mind flipping cuddling up to him at night, I can tell you."

Doris gave a little gasp, then furiously attacked the potato, while Mrs. Chubb shook her head in disgust. "Gertie Brown, how dare you talk like that. You the mother of two precious babies and all."

"Don't mean I'm a bleeding nun, though, does it? Ain't no harm in bloody looking, that's what I say." She picked up the tray of silverware and marched to the door. "Who'd be a bleeding woman, I ask you? The blinking men have all the fun while the women end up flipping lumbered. The bloody trouble is, once you've done it and you don't have it anymore, you bloody miss it."

She thoroughly enjoyed the shocked silence she left behind her as she passed through the door.

"I do not understand this entry here," Malcolm Ridlington said, jabbing the nib of his pen at the neatly inscribed figures in the ledger. "It makes no sense to me at all."

Cecily peered at the upside-down figures, trying to make them out. She was reluctant to move around the desk to look over Malcolm's shoulder. Fortunately the manager swiveled the ledger around so that she could get a better look.

"Here," he said irritably, tapping his pen at the entry again. He left behind a minute spot of black ink, and Cecily frowned.

Doing her best to curb her irritation, she said pleasantly, "Ah, that is the sum I paid Ben Parkinson for the work he did on the roof."

"And what is this entry up here, then, pray?"

Cecily peered closer. "That is the bill for the supplies for the roof."

"Then perhaps you will kindly explain why the two figures are not in the same column?"

Cecily straightened. "One figure is for supplies, the other is payment for work done. Baxter always—"

Malcolm rudely snatched the ledger away from her and switched it around again. "I am not particularly interested in your ex-manager's procedures, madam. From what I can tell, his methods of accounting were decidedly haphazard."

This time she could not stand by and allow this unpleasant man to malign Baxter in such an appalling manner. "Baxter's methods, like the man himself, were impeccable," she told him. "If the accounts are inaccurate, then you must find fault with me, not my ex-manager."

Apparently aware that he had overstepped the line, Malcolm's irate expression faded into one of resignation. "I realize, madam, that you are no expert at these matters. I will do my best to sort out this atrocious muddle. I fear, however, that it will take some time to repair the damage."

"Take all the time you need, Mr. Ridlington. I will attempt to perform some of your other duties so that you might concentrate on the problem."

Malcolm actually looked relieved. "Thank you, madam. That will be much appreciated."

"Not at all." Cecily left him poring over the ledger, resentment burning in her soul. It was true, she had not had much experience in accounting. She was reasonably intelligent, however, and the system that Baxter had used was not that complicated.

Admittedly, the accounts had been sadly neglected, but they couldn't be as bad as Malcolm Ridlington suggested. The man was making a mountain out of a molehill, for heaven's sake.

Making her way to the lobby, Cecily felt a strong urge to ask Baxter to help out with the accounts. She could not do that, of course. In the first place, she was quite sure that Malcolm would resent any interference from his predecessor. In the second place, she was reluctant to let Baxter know how inefficient she was and how badly she needed him.

In any case, he had made no mention of seeing her again. For all she knew, Baxter could very well depart for London again without bothering to pay her another visit. The thought would have depressed her were she not nursing the conviction that Baxter had every intention of returning to the Pennyfoot. Though just when that would be was every bit as unpredictable as the summer weather.

Reaching the lobby, Cecily saw her new doorman open the main door for a departing guest with a sweeping flourish that looked most proficient.

Catching sight of her, Ned Harris closed the door again and touched the bill of his peaked cap as he gave her a slight bow. "Mornin', Mrs. Sinclair. How am I doing, then?"

"Quite well, by all accounts." Cecily smiled at him. "I hope you are happy working at the Pennyfoot?"

"Oh, indeed I am, mum. Couldn't be better."

"I'm glad to hear it." She looked him over with a critical eye. "The uniform appears to fit quite well."

Ned nodded with cheerful enthusiasm. "Everything except the titfer. Bit large that were, 'til I stuffed paper in it."

Cecily frowned. "Titfer?"

"Tit for tat." Ned pointed to his cap. "Me hat, mum."

"Then why didn't you say so?" She gave him a stern look. "I hope you haven't forgotten your promise to refrain from using those slang expressions."

"Oh, no, mum, I haven't forgot, honest." Ned flashed his engaging grin. "Sometimes I forget, like. It just sort of slips out. I am getting better at it, though. Mark my words, mum, in a day or two I'll have forgotten I was ever a cockney from Bow."

"You should never forget your heritage, Ned." Cecily stepped toward the door and waited for him to open it. "All I ask is that you speak so that people can understand you."

"I will do that, Mrs. S, I promise you. And Ned Harris always keeps a promise. You can bet your daisy roots . . . er . . . boots on that."

Sighing, Cecily made her way down the steps of the hotel. Samuel waited for her at the curb, holding the reins of the chestnut. He sprang forward as she approached and tipped his cap.

"Take me to St. Bartholomew's, Samuel," Cecily ordered as she climbed into the trap.

"Yes, mum." Samuel waited for her to seat herself on the leather seat before clambering up to his seat in front of her.

Cecily relaxed as the trap moved away from the curb and began to head down the Esplanade. The fresh sea breeze tugged at her navy hat, which she had secured with three hat pins and a pale pink scarf tied under her chin.

The sun felt quite warm on her back, even though a faint mist hovered over the sea. Already the sands were crowded with visitors, many of them surrounding the red-and-white-striped tent of the Punch and Judy show.

Delicate lace-trimmed parasols bobbed up and down as ladies strolled with their escorts along the water's edge, sidestepping every now and then to avoid the sand castles, while the shrill voices of children mingled with the hungry cries of the seagulls.

Seasons came and went so swiftly, Cecily thought, switching her gaze to the row of little shops along the Esplanade. It was hard to believe that already it was 1909. The Prince of Wales had been on the throne more than eight years. She could remember Queen Victoria's death as clearly as if it were yesterday. How swiftly life flew by without one's noticing its passing.

Yet sometimes it seemed as if the past three months had lasted for years. How she missed seeing Baxter every day, teasing him, conspiring with him and on rare occasions, even quarrelling with him.

He had become so much a part of her life since James had died, and she had more or less taken him for granted—until he was no longer there for her, giving her gentle support and understanding whenever she lapsed into moods such as this one.

Stirring herself, Cecily reminded herself of her blessings. She was alive and healthy. Not like poor Will Jones, who would never again gaze upon the grassy slopes of Putney Downs under a misty blue sky. She had a lot to be thankful for, she told herself sternly. And if life didn't offer her all that she would wish, she was at least fortunate to have a comfortable home and friends who cared about her.

Settling her back against the leather seat, she let her mind dwell on the sharp tattoo of the chestnut's hooves, the creaking of springs beneath the trap, and the sound of children's laughter floating on a salty sea breeze.

In spite of her efforts, however, she could not prevent the image forming in her mind of an old man's broken body lying on the rocks of Devil's Cauldron.

Poor Phoebe must be in a state of shock and would need a calm mind and a comforting voice to soothe her shattered nerves. Cecily could only hope that she could forget her own troubles and rise to the occasion.

CHAPTER

❈ 4 ❈

Colonel Frederick Fortescue was not an early riser. There were several reasons why not. First and foremost, his nightly jaunts to the local pub, the George and Dragon Inn, more often than not rendered him quite tipsy. Therefore it took him more than half the night to find his way back to the Pennyfoot Hotel.

His head usually remained befuddled until midmorning, when his body went into alcohol withdrawal, shocking his distorted mind into a vague awakening. The aftereffects of being within close earshot of rifle fire during the Boer War only complicated matters.

In fact, even at the best of times, most acquaintances of the portly gentleman considered him more than a little short on ammunition.

All in all, Colonel Fortescue was not at his best until he had downed his midday shot of gin. He was on his way to take care of that urgent matter when he happened to collide, quite literally, with Ned Harris, who was dashing across the lobby at the time.

The colonel, whose vast belly supplied an admirable cushion for Ned's agile body, promptly lost all of his breath when the doorman plowed into him. It was several moments before he recovered it, while Ned anxiously hovered over him.

"Sorry, mate, I didn't see you coming round the jolly Jack, did I. Are you all right, then? Can I get you a nice cup of Rosie?"

The colonel leaned against the carved oak banisters of the staircase and struggled to breathe. The humming in his head gradually subsided as oxygen filtered back into his brain.

He peered at the strange young man standing over him and said hoarsely, "What did you say, old chap? Didn't quite catch that."

"I asked you if you wanted a cup of Rosie." The doorman grinned. "Rosie Lee. Tea."

"Quite, quite." The colonel's eyelids started flapping up and down at an alarming rate, seriously affecting his vision. "I have no blasted idea what you're talking about, old bean. Have to speak more slowly, you know. Dashed hard to understand, otherwise, what?"

"Sorry, guv, I keep forgetting." Ned pursed his lips and said very slowly and distinctly, "Would you like a cup of tea, sir?"

"Oh that! By Jove, now I understand." Fortescue gave the suggestion some serious consideration. "Don't think so, old boy," he said at last. "I'm on my way to get a drop of mother's ruin."

Ned shuddered. "Gin? Can't abide the stuff meself. Give

me a good drop of wallop any time. Builds me muscles up, it does."

"Wallop? Can't say I've heard of that, old chap. Some sort of whiskey, is it?"

"He means beer, Colonel," Gertie's voice said behind him.

The colonel swung around, then steadied himself as the lobby kept spinning for a moment or two. "Does he, by George? Never heard it called that before."

"You promised you wouldn't use that bloody slang," Gertie said to Ned.

"Sorry, luv. I forgot."

"Oh, slang, is it? Now I understand." The colonel nodded his head up and down. "Yes, by thunder, I know all about slang. Used it in India, you know. Oh, yes, all the time. Can't remember a dashed word of it now, of course."

"Is that where you got that spiffy whistle?"

"Suit," Gertie said, scowling at Ned.

"Yeah, that's what I said, luv. Whistle and flute . . . suit."

"You're doing that on bloody purpose." Gertie dug her fists into her hips. "I'll tell on you, Ned Harris, if you don't bleeding behave."

Fortescue looked from one to the other. He had not the faintest idea what they were talking about. Nor did he care to know. Right then, all he could think about was the cool, refreshing taste of a good dry martini. "Well, I'd best be off, then," he muttered.

Neither Gertie nor the young man so much as turned their heads. They were gazing at each other like a pair of lovesick cows. Fortescue wasted no more time on them. Muttering to himself, he tottered off down the hallway in the direction of the hotel bar.

Gertie barely noticed him leave. She was too busy trying

to gauge the twinkle in Ned Harris's eye. She'd been burned once before by a pair of laughing eyes. Much as she liked the looks of the new doorman, a little voice in her head told her that he couldn't be trusted. And Gertie wasn't about to ignore that little voice.

"You're looking very chipper this morning," Ned said, running his eye over her gray striped dress and apron with a boldness that made her blush.

"I can't stand here all day talking to the likes of you," she said, putting on her prim look. "Mrs. Chubb will have my guts for garters, that she will."

Ned assumed an innocent expression. "Well, go on, then, darlin'. I'm not keeping you now, am I?"

Gertie tossed her head. "You'd better watch your tongue, Ned Harris, if you want to keep this job."

His hearty laugh rang out across the lobby. "Don't worry, luv. I don't expect to be here for very long, anyway."

Wondering what he meant by that, Gertie left him still chuckling. There were times when she didn't understand him at all. And it had nothing to do with cockney slang.

The trap jerked to a halt at the entrance to the church, and Cecily, more out of habit than anything, straightened her hat before allowing Samuel to help her down. "I don't know how long I shall be, Samuel, so if you have errands to run, please do so. As long as I am back at the hotel before the midday meal is over, I don't mind waiting for you to return for me."

"Yes, mum, thank you, mum." Samuel took off his cap and crushed it in his hands. "I do have to go into town to order some more feed, and Michel asked me to bring back some more brandy from the George and Dragon."

"Very well, I shall wait for you, then." That settled, she made her way up the driveway to the church porch.

She heard the voices the minute she pushed the door open. They echoed in the empty church—the shrill, high-pitched prattle from Phoebe, Algie's feeble stuttering, and the slow, monotonous voice of P.C. Northcott.

The constable must have arrived shortly before her, Cecily thought as she walked down the carpeted aisle toward the little group standing in front of the pews. He was still asking the obvious questions.

"What time would you say that were, Mrs. Carter-Holmes?"

Phoebe lifted a hand to clutch her slender throat. "I told you, Constable, it must have been close to eight o'clock last night. As you well know, Will always rang the bells at half past seven, for the evening service."

"There was no s-service last night," Algie said, his pale eyes looking wider than usual behind his spectacles. "It was Saint B-bartholomew's Feast last night at the Pennyfoot." Catching sight of Cecily approaching, the vicar greeted her with a nervous nod of his head. "H-hello, Mrs. Sinclair. Good of you to come."

P.C. Northcott looked up with a frown of annoyance at this interruption while Phoebe swung around with a glad cry.

"Oh, Cecily dear, I didn't hear you coming. Such a tragedy. Poor, poor Will." She twisted a lace handkerchief into a ball and delicately dabbed at her eyes. "He had been with us for so long. It's like losing one of the family."

"There, there, mother," Algie said, patting her shoulder. "Don't . . . ah . . . take on so."

"I'm so sorry, Phoebe," Cecily murmured, knowing that her friend's grief was genuine. She had been very fond of Will. Glancing at the constable, she added, "Is there anything I can do to help?"

Northcott puffed out his chest, threatening to burst the

buttons on his straining uniform jacket. Lifting a pencil to his lips, he darted his tongue over the end of it, then poised it over the crumpled pad in his hand. "Not h'unless you were on Putney Downs h'in the vicinity of Devil's Cauldron around eight o'clock last night."

"I was having dinner in the hotel at that time," Cecily said quietly.

"So I've been told, ma'am."

"Poor Will must have come down to ring the bells as usual," Phoebe said mournfully. "He must have lost his footing on the way home." She permitted a small sob to escape her trembling lips. "He was getting old, you know. I noticed lately that he was becoming quite frail. I wondered how much longer he'd be able to climb the steps to the belfry. I never expected anything like this to happen to him."

Her voice had trembled badly on the last two words, and Cecily moved closer to put a comforting arm around her. "This must be a dreadful shock for you, Phoebe. I am so sorry."

The constable closed his notebook with an official-sounding snap. "Yes, well, since there doesn't seem much that anyone can tell me, I will simply report this h'unfortunate accident to Inspector Cranshaw. If he wants any more information, I will let you know."

"I really don't know what else we c-can tell you," Algie said, sliding his glasses further up his nose. "We were all at the . . . ah . . . feast last night."

"Yes, well, some of us weren't so fortunate," Northcott said, giving Cecily a sly look out of the corner of his eye. "Someone might have seen Will fall off the cliff."

"If someone had," Cecily said, ignoring the constable's dig, "surely he or she would have reported it last night?"

The constable shrugged. "One would think so, Mrs.

Sinclair. One would certainly think so." He touched the brim of his policeman's helmet. "Good day to you, ladies. And to you, Vicar."

Algie nodded, while Phoebe sniffed loudly and dabbed once more at her nose.

"Don't bother to see me out," Northcott said as Algie moved forward. "I know my way." He trudged off up the aisle as if he carried the weight of the universe on his pudgy shoulders.

Phoebe sank down onto the front pew with a trembling sigh. "This is a horrible thing to happen. Horrible. This week of all weeks. Who will ring the church bells tonight?"

"I will have to, of course," Algie said, looking aghast at the thought. "We can't break the tradition, what with the b-bishop here. It wouldn't be right."

Phoebe peeked up at him. "Thank you, dear. I knew you'd think of something."

"We shall have to find another . . . ah . . . bell ringer as soon as possible," Algie said with a worried frown. "I'll ask for a volunteer at the service tonight."

"That's a good idea." Phoebe sniffed again. "Though no one will be able to take the place of poor Will."

Cecily sat down next to her and patted her hand. As she did so, her glance fell upon the chalice standing in regal splendor next to the alter. Her soft exclamation brought a smile to Algie's face as he followed her gaze.

"Quite m-magnificent, isn't it?" he murmured. "I still can't believe it is actually under the roof of my church. I have to keep looking at it to convince myself I didn't . . . ah . . . dream it."

"It is beautiful." Cecily stood and moved closer to take a better look. The rubies and emeralds glowed against the bright gold background, so large they didn't look real. "It must be worth a great deal of money."

"Oh, priceless, of course." Algie came to stand next to her. "It's very old, you know."

"Yes," Cecily murmured, "so I heard."

"Oh, really, Algie," Phoebe said plaintively. "How can you go on babbling about that silly chalice when poor Will—" Her voice broke off in a sob.

Algie looked affronted. "S-silly? I hope you won't let the b-bishop hear you say that."

"Oh, you know what I mean." Phoebe heaved a loud sigh. "I suppose it's just as well he lived alone. At least he didn't leave someone worrying all night about him. Now there is no one to mourn him except me."

"I say, Mother, that's not . . . ah . . . cricket. I'll mourn him, too."

"When you're not gazing at that silly chalice," Phoebe muttered.

"I have some time to wait for Samuel to return," Cecily said hurriedly. "Perhaps we could retire to the vicarage for a nice cup of tea? I think it would make you feel better."

Phoebe dabbed at her eyes one more time, then rose. "I suppose you're right, Cecily. Somehow a hot cup of tea always works wonders. Come, let us go to the vicarage, and I'll tell you about my plans for the clipping on Friday."

Relieved, Cecily followed her from the church, leaving Algie alone once more to enjoy his precious chalice.

The door of the kitchen flew open, startling Gertie, who stood at one end of the table folding serviettes. Mrs. Chubb looked up from the other end, where she was kneading pastry.

Doris stood in the doorway, her face flushed, her mouth opening and shutting like a goldfish.

"What's the bleeding matter with you?" Gertie demanded. "You look like you seen the devil hisself."

"I have," Doris gasped. "It's that awful man, Mr. Barker." Her voice rose to a wail. "I hate him!"

Gertie dropped the serviette and dug her fists into her hips. "Why? What'd he do to you?"

Doris burst into tears. "He tried to . . . kiss me! His breath was all smelly and minty, and he pushed me up against a wall."

Mrs. Chubb tutted and shook her head in disgust.

"Is that all?" Gertie shook her head. "You have to bleeding get used to that. Lots of bloody men tries it."

"I don't want them to try it with me!" Doris wailed louder.

"There, there," Mrs. Chubb said. "Don't take on, duck. No harm was done, I'm sure."

"*Sacre bleu!*" Michel exclaimed from the stove, his tall white chef's hat bobbing with his indignation. "Once again I 'ave to wait for ze eggs for ze crème brûlée. Everyone expect me to create a masterpiece, *n'est-ce pas?* Tell me how I do that when I am surrounded by nincoompops, *oui?*"

Gertie winced as a saucepan lid clattered on the red tiled floor of the kitchen. "Nincompoops, you bloody twit," she muttered under her breath. Although she knew that Michel's mangling of the English language was as big a pretense as his fake French accent, he still managed to irritate her whenever he did it.

"Get Michel his eggs, will you, duck?" Mrs. Chubb said kindly as Doris stood there wiping her eyes with her sleeve.

Doris nodded and headed for the pantry, still sniffing.

Gertie's fingers flew as she expertly folded the serviettes into the shape of a fan. Across the kitchen a loud howl caught everyone's attention. Gertie's head shot up in alarm.

Her nine-month-old son sat on a blanket under the window, banging his sister on the head with a wooden spoon. Lillian's face was bright red, and her mouth formed a perfect circle as she let out an ear-splitting scream.

Daisy, who had been arranging chairs around the babies in the futile hope of keeping them confined, dropped to her knees and gently took the spoon away from James. Then she lifted Lillian onto her lap, where the child stuffed a small fist inside her mouth, mercifully smothering her cries.

"Mon Dieu!" Michel muttered. "If it's not ze women cackling and crying, it's ze babies screaming."

Gertie sent a guilty glance at Mrs. Chubb, who was ordering Doris to take the covered dishes of poached salmon to the dining room. The kitchen seemed to be a bloody state of bedlam, Gertie thought, and her two nippers weren't making it any easier.

Having finished with Doris, Mrs. Chubb disappeared into the pantry. Daisy, having comforted Lillian, was trying to fill the salt and pepper shakers while keeping a watchful eye on the babies. James, having become bored with the spoon, had pulled himself up on his feet and clung precariously to the chair, a proud grin on his chubby face.

Any minute now, Gertie thought gloomily, he was going to stick out a foot and attempt to walk through the gap in the chairs. She just bleeding hoped one of them could stop him before he got under someone's feet. Of course, then he'd start bloody howling if he couldn't go where he wanted to go.

Mrs. Chubb came hurrying out of the pantry, carrying two huge blackberry and apple pies. "Gertie? Are you finished with those serviettes? Get them on the table as fast as you can. It's almost time to ring the dinner gong."

"Yes, Mrs. Chubb." Piling the serviettes on a large tea tray, Gertie took a last anxious look at her babies, then charged out of the kitchen with the tray. She couldn't watch them all the time, she told herself as she rushed up the stairs.

That was Daisy's job. Only Daisy had work to do as well. What she needed was a bleeding full-time nanny.

Flying down the hallway to the dining room, Gertie had to laugh at herself. Only toffs could afford nannies. Bloody nannies earned more money than she did. Somehow she'd have to manage with the babies. She could hardly leave the poor blighters locked up in her tiny room all day. They'd end up as bleeding barmy as Colonel Fortescue if she did that.

Doris met her in the doorway. "Here," Gertie panted, "shove these on the flipping tables for me, will you? I've got to get back to the blinking kitchen."

Doris took the tray with a willing smile, and Gertie silently blessed her. She could always count on Doris to help. In fact, she didn't know what she'd do without the twins. All this rushing about was getting her down, she thought as she sped back to the kitchen. Too much more of this and she'd be old before her time.

Rushing into the kitchen, her first thought was for the babies. To her immense relief she saw them sitting quietly on the blanket, while Lillian watched James try to fit a lid onto the saucepan someone had given him.

Mrs. Chubb greeted her with a frown. "Where have you been, Gertie? Michel is waiting for you to grate the lemons."

"Cor, strewth, Mrs. Chubb, I just got bleeding back from the dining room. I ran all the bloody way, I did."

The housekeeper nodded irritably. "Yes, yes. Well, get on with those lemons, then, there's a good girl. And when that's done, the potatoes will need mashing."

"I've only got one flipping pair of hands." Gertie stomped over to the larder to get the lemons. "If you ask me, we need some more bleeding help in here. Bunch of greedy buggers they are out there. Gobble up everything in sight, they do."

"That's what they pay for," Mrs. Chubb said crisply, "and

it's not our place to criticize. So I'll ask you to keep a civil tongue in your head, my girl."

"That ees humanly eempossible," Michel declared, slapping butter into a sizzling-hot pan.

At that precise moment a piercing shriek drowned out everything else. Spinning around, Gertie saw James struggling with the saucepan, which was upside down on his head.

Daisy gave a cry and dropped to her knees. "I only took my eyes off them for second," she said as she eased the pot from James's squalling face.

"Oh, good heavens," Mrs. Chubb said crossly. "What next?"

Too blooming true, what next, Gertie thought. She was close to tears herself.

She didn't hear the kitchen door open, but the familiar voice seemed to ring in her ears.

"Well, I can see things haven't changed that much since I left," a slender young woman said from the doorway.

Gertie's eyes opened wide. "Ethel!" she cried, and promptly burst into tears.

CHAPTER

❈ 5 ❈

Jogging along the Esplanade in the trap once more, Cecily couldn't help dwelling on Phoebe's words concerning the lack of mourners for Will Jones. Although the bell ringer had spent a good deal of time at the church, taking care of the maintenance and tending to the gardens, few people spoke to him.

He was, in fact, rather like a painting. After a while one was so used to seeing it on the wall that it no longer had much significance.

Much like James Sinclair's portrait.

Uncomfortable with that reflection, Cecily directed her thoughts back to Will. It saddened her to think that he had died in such a lonely spot and all alone. Those last seconds of his life must have been terrifying. She could just imagine him stumbling, trying to regain his footing, then plunging down to the jagged rocks below.

In spite of the warm sun, she felt a shiver down her back. It was never pleasant to dwell on death, but to die so needlessly, because of a misplaced step, seemed such a terrible tragedy. Maybe that was why the accident weighed so heavily on her mind. Or perhaps it was the depression that never left her for very long before returning to cloak her spirits and bog them down.

With a determined lift of her chin, Cecily pushed aside her morbid thoughts. In the distance she could see the sun sparkling on the white walls of the Pennyfoot. People crammed the shops along the Esplanade, spilling out of doorways and peering into the leaded bay windows.

A brilliant yellow motor car chugged past the trap, leaving a trail of evil-smelling smoke. The chestnut tossed his head as if in disgust, and Samuel flicked the reins, reminding the horse who was in charge.

How fortunate she was, Cecily reminded herself, to have so many dear friends. Even though her family was departed, with her husband dead and her sons abroad, her surrogate family, the staff of the Pennyfoot, amply filled the void. She could ask for nothing more.

She would not think about Baxter, nor would she pin any false hopes on the fact that he was in Badgers End. Whatever his intentions were, it was unlikely they concerned her.

In fact, she was beginning to wish he had never returned. She had been on the point of banishing him from her mind altogether, until his precipitous appearance in the roof garden. The man was exasperating as always. And as unpredictable as ever.

Fortunately for her peace of mind, the trap drew up in front of the hotel steps. Cecily waited for Samuel to clamber down and offer her an arm, though she was quite capable of alighting from her seat herself. She was in no mood to assert her independence, however. In fact, she hadn't bothered to do so in some time. Since Baxter had left, in fact.

The thought troubled her. So much so that she didn't see Colonel Fortescue until he blocked her path at the top of the stairs.

"What ho, old girl! Been for a stroll, have we, what?"

Detecting the strong smell of gin, Cecily retreated a couple of paces. "I've been to the church, Colonel. I'm afraid one of our parishioners has met with an accident."

"Oh, sorry to hear that, old bean. Anyone I know?"

"Will Jones, the bell ringer. Were you acquainted with him, Colonel?"

"Can't say that I was, madam. Not dead, is he?"

"I'm afraid he is, yes."

"Oh, dashed bad luck that, what?" The colonel loudly cleared his throat. "Must pay my condolences to the widow."

"Will Jones wasn't married, Colonel," Cecily said gently.

Fortescue looked confused. "He wasn't? Then how the devil did he leave a widow?"

"He didn't." Cecily sighed, wondering why she persisted in attempting a normal conversation with the colonel when she knew perfectly well that such a thing was impossible. "If you'll excuse me, Colonel, I—"

"Jolly uncivil of him if you ask me," Fortescue muttered.

"Quite. Now if you'll—"

"Reminds me of a chappie in India. Introduced this lady as his wife. Took her everywhere—military balls, polo matches, band concerts. Everywhere he blasted went, so did she."

"Yes, that is most interesting indeed, Colonel, but I really—"

"Then one night, he was dancing with her in the officers' mess, when this burly fellow charged into the room, waving a saber and bellowing like a wounded elephant."

Cecily nodded politely and tried to sidestep around him. The colonel moved with her, still blocking her way.

"Everyone scattered, of course. Thought it was someone gone mad. Did that a lot, you know, in the tropics. Too blasted hot for a lot of them. Got them down in the end."

"I'm sure it must have—"

"Anyway, turns out the chap was the woman's rightful husband. Sliced the other chap's head clean off. By George, I never saw—"

Afraid that the colonel was about to embark on the gory details, Cecily said loudly, "I don't remember seeing you at the feast last night, Colonel. I hope you enjoyed the meal?"

Fortescue blinked rapidly. "Feast?"

"St. Bartholomew's Feast," Cecily said gently. "In the dining room last night. Perhaps you remember the boar's head being carried in? Or you must remember the flaming plum puddings?"

The colonel's head jerked back. "I say, old girl. Not used to hearing you curse, you know."

"I didn't curse, Colonel. I merely meant that the plum puddings were in flames."

"Good God! Hope someone was able to put them out. Must have been a nasty business. Do any damage, did they?"

Cecily gave up. "No, Colonel. No damage. Now if you'll excuse me—"

"Must have missed that, by Jove. Completely forgot about it. Old St. Bartholomew's Feast, eh? Can't imagine how I could have forgotten that."

He was beginning to look distressed, and Cecily did her

best to comfort him. "Perhaps you just forgot you were there," she said kindly.

The colonel gave his head an emphatic shake. "No, no, old bean. I remember distinctly, I was down at the George and Dragon last night." He frowned. "Dashed peculiar, that."

"Well, never mind, Colonel. We'll be having another one next year."

He blinked at her again. "What? Oh, that. Jolly good show." He heaved an enormous sigh. "I must be slowing down, old girl. Must be the old ticker, you know. Not what it used to be, I'm afraid."

"I'm sorry to hear that, Colonel."

"Yes, well, happens to all of us, I suppose." His face took on the expression of a wounded bloodhound. "Took me an extra fifteen minutes to reach the pub last night. Can you imagine? Fifteen minutes late for my nip of brandy. Funny thing was, my blasted feet seemed to be keeping up the usual pace. Just goes to show, what, what?"

"Yes, indeed." Cecily wasn't quite sure what was supposed to show what. She wasn't about to discuss it, however. Smiling, she managed to skirt around the somber gentleman. Pulling on the bell rope, she prayed Ned would be quick in opening the door.

"Oh, I say, old bean," the colonel said, then looked around as if wondering where she had gone. "Oh, there you are. Just wanted to thank you for those spiffing chocolate mint sweets I found in my room. Dashed delicious, they are. Can't leave them alone, by Jove."

"I'm glad you like them, Colonel. It's our special treat to the guests in honor of the celebrations this week." To Cecily's relief, the door opened behind her. "I hope you enjoy your day," she added, before deliberately turning her back and stepping into the foyer.

Ned greeted her cheerfully and closed the door, leaving Cecily feeling just a little guilty for having deserted the colonel in such an abrupt manner. There were times, however, when a hasty escape was necessary if she wanted to hold onto her own sanity.

"There's a gentleman waiting for you in the library, mum," Ned said as she was about to cross the lobby.

"Gentleman?" Try as she might, she could not ignore the sudden leap of expectation. "Did he leave his card?"

"Yes, mum." Ned handed it to her with a flourish. "I suggested he wait in the drawing room, but he said he preferred the library. I hope I did all right?"

Cecily stared down at Baxter's card, trying to compose the silly fluttering under her ribs. "Yes, of course, Ned. Thank you."

She walked slowly across the wide Axminster carpet, aware of Ned's curious gaze on her back. Although her feet felt as if they were floating inches above the floor, she was determined not to hurry.

It would do Baxter good to wait for her, she thought. Besides, she needed time to settle her ruffled nerves. She wanted to appear calm and composed for this meeting. If that were at all possible.

"I can't believe it's really you," Gertie said, wiping her nose on the back of her sleeve.

Ethel laughed. "It's not very often I can pull one over on you, Gertie Brown. I couldn't wait to see your face when you saw me. I was going to come yesterday, but then I remembered about the feast. I thought I'd better wait until today."

She came forward into the kitchen, and Gertie looked her up and down. She looked a little fatter than when Gertie last saw her, and she was wearing one of the latest frocks that everyone was talking about. It had broad stripes of dark pink running down the lighter pink material, and had no lace or ribbon on it anywhere. Not even a ruffle.

The skirt was much narrower than Gertie was used to seeing, with no flounces at all, and actually seemed tight at the hips. The hem barely skimmed the pointed toes of Ethel's buttoned boots. Also, Gertie noticed with envy, Ethel's corset wasn't cinched in tightly at the waist. She'd heard about the latest fashion of looser corsets.

"You look bleeding dapper," she said as Ethel paused in front of her.

"She does, indeed," Mrs. Chubb agreed, coming forward to inspect the new arrival. "It's nice to see you again, duck. How's London treating you, then? Very well, by the look of those nice clothes."

Michel uttered a loud groan. "Is this a kitchen or a fashion show? Where the 'eck are my lemons, s'il vous plaît?"

"Oh, keep your bleeding hair on," Gertie muttered.

Ethel took the lemons from her. "I'll do the lemons for you, Michel. It's nice to see you again."

Michel grunted, but his frown vanished.

"How long can you stay?" Mrs. Chubb asked, wiping her hands on her apron. "I'm really busy right now with the meal, but I would love to hear about London."

"I'll be around for a while," Ethel said, grinning at Gertie, who still had trouble believing her old friend was actually standing there in the kitchen. "I'll help Gertie while we talk. Then Michel can't yell at me."

Michel answered that with a disdainful toss of his head.

"He bloody yells at everyone nowadays," Gertie said, handing Ethel the grater. "No one takes any bleeding notice of him, though."

"You will take notice of me if I slap you with ze wet kipper," Michel muttered.

"Here, child," Mrs. Chubb said, taking a white garment from the dresser drawer. "If you're going to help, and Lord knows we could do with it, you'd better put this apron on. Can't have you spoiling those nice clothes, that we can't. Madam would never forgive us."

Ethel dropped the lemons onto the table and tied the apron around her. "Feels like old times," she said, looking around the kitchen. "Doesn't seem like a year since I was working here."

A loud babble came from the corner of the kitchen, and Ethel swung around to look. James was once more on his feet, peeking over the seat of the chair at the newcomer.

"Oh, my," Ethel said breathlessly. "I'd forgotten about the babies in all the excitement." She rushed forward and dropped to her knees by the chairs. "Oh, Gertie, they are just so precious."

Gertie felt a rush of warmth and pride. "They're a bleeding nuisance, that's what," she said, trying not to sound like a doting mother.

"They're not a nuisance," Daisy said sharply. "They just need lots of attention, that's all."

"You'd better bloody watch out for Daisy." Gertie laughed. "She won't let no one bleeding say anything bad about the babies."

Ethel looked up and smiled. "I'm Ethel," she said. "I used to work here."

Daisy gave her a tight nod. "I know. I heard about you from Miss Brown."

"Yeah, I told her about all the bloody tricks we used to get up to and all."

Ethel gave both babies a pat on the head, then got to her feet. "I miss those times," she said wistfully.

"Cor, strewth, so do I," Gertie said with feeling.

"Oh, 'ow my heart bleeds for you," Michel said, holding

a hand over his heart. "Someone else is going to bleed, however, if I do not have my lemons in ten seconds."

"Oops, I forgot." Ethel scurried over to the table and starting frantically grating a lemon. The sharp citrus smell sweetened the air, and Gertie smiled happily at her friend.

"So what are you blinking doing down here, then?" she demanded as she added butter and cream to a large, steaming pot of boiled potatoes.

A fit of coughing prevented Ethel from answering right away. "Well, me and Joe got tired of living in the Smoke," she said, her voice croaking. She finished one lemon and started on the next. "All that dirt and noise and everything. We kept missing the sea and the fields and all the trees. Then Joe heard about this farm that was going really cheap, and he came down to take a look at it. He still had a bit of money left from the sale of his farm last year, so he bought it."

Gertie dropped the fork she was holding. "You mean it? You and Joe are going to bloody live back here, then?"

Ethel grinned. "I thought you'd be happy to hear that."

Gertie clutched the fork to her bosom. "I haven't been this 'appy since me nippers were bloody born."

Ethel finished grating the lemon and licked her fingers. Screwing up her face at the acid taste, she said, "Do you think madam will give me my job back?"

"Mercy me," Michel said with a groan.

"Oh, Gawd, Ethel, that would be flipping marvelous." Gertie shivered with glee. "Just imagine the two of us back together again."

"What's that?" Mrs. Chubb asked, bustling out of the pantry. "Did I hear Ethel say she wanted her job back?"

"What you heard," Michel said heavily, "was the voice of catastrof. These two . . . 'ow you say . . . scoundrels, are planning to invade the Pennyfoot once more."

"Catastrophe," Mrs. Chubb murmured. "I do wish you'd learn to speak proper English, Michel."

"He can bleeding speak it proper enough when he's flipping knocked back half a bottle of blinking brandy," Gertie said darkly.

Ethel giggled.

Michel answered by dropping a saucepan onto the floor.

Both babies immediately started howling, and both Daisy and Ethel rushed to console them, while Gertie went on mashing potatoes.

"I must admit," Mrs. Chubb said, smoothing back a stray wisp of gray hair that had escaped her cap, "I would welcome another pair of hands. We simply don't have enough help to cope with all this extra work."

"There will not be any need to worry," Michel said, his voice rising on a dangerous note, "because there will not be any guests. They will all starve to death if I do not get my lemons this eenstant!"

Once more Ethel jumped to her feet. "I'm going as fast as I can," she said plaintively.

Gertie lifted her head and sighed with satisfaction. "Just like old times."

"Well, don't get too excited about it," Mrs. Chubb warned. "I don't know if madam will be able to hire Ethel again. What with the money situation, and all. She has the twins' wages to find, as well as Ned Harris's."

"She doesn't have to bleeding pay Mr. Baxter anymore," Gertie said, determined not to let her dream slip away. She hadn't realized how much she'd missed Ethel until she'd seen her right there at the kitchen table, working with her just as she used to do.

Ethel looked up in surprise. "Mr. Baxter's working for free?"

Gertie laughed. "Not bleeding likely. He's left, that's what. Been gone three blinking months now."

"You're forgetting the new manager," Mrs. Chubb reminded her.

Gertie's face fell. "Oh, yeah, him."

"You got a new manager? What's he like?"

Gertie shrugged. "Don't know. I haven't spoke to him yet."

"He seems like a very nice gentleman," Mrs. Chubb said loyally. "He used to be with a countess in Scotland, so I believe."

"Ooo, fancy that," Ethel said.

"Well, I bet he ain't bleeding like Mr. Baxter." Gertie laid down her fork and picked up the pot of mashed potatoes. "I bet madam wishes she had him back. I always thought she bleeding fancied him."

"Gertie Brown!" Mrs. Chubb crossed her arms over her abundant breasts. "How dare you talk about madam in that disgusting manner!"

Gertie dumped the pot of potatoes back on the stove. "I only said as how she bloody fancied him. I didn't say they was up to any blinking hanky-panky."

She waited until Mrs. Chubb had disappeared into the pantry again before turning to Ethel with a broad wink. "Mind you, if it was me, I'd be wishing there *was* some hanky panky. For an old gent, that Mr. Baxter is a bleeding bit of all right."

"Yeah," Ethel said, carrying the plate of grated lemon peel over to Michel, "I can't believe he left. I bet madam misses him."

"Not 'alf. Though I heard he was back last night. Samuel said he was in the bloody dining room with madam, having dinner."

"Ooo, fancy that." Ethel went over to the sink and rinsed her hands. "Do you think he came back for his job, too?"

"I don't know," Gertie said thoughtfully. "But I wouldn't be at all surprised if he came back for something bleeding important."

"Like what?" Ethel asked, her eyes wide with expectation.

Gertie shrugged. "How the 'ell should I know? I reckon we'll bloody find out, though, soon enough."

CHAPTER

6

Pausing at the door to the library, Cecily stole a moment to catch her breath. The ridiculous thumping in her breast showed no signs of abating, no matter how sternly she scolded herself. The very first chance she got, she decided, she'd ask Baxter for one of his cigars. Smoking one of them always calmed her down.

She grasped the handle of the door and squared her shoulders. Then, taking care to paste a bright smile upon her face, she pushed the door open and entered the library.

He was standing at the French windows, gazing out at the thick, leafy arches of rambling roses. His hands were clasped behind his back, and he appeared to be in deep thought, for it was a moment or two before he turned his head.

His smile took her breath away. He had so rarely smiled when he'd worked for her. Not that he was unhappy, or at least for the most part, so she believed. In his position as employee, Baxter had deemed it improper to smile, unless the occasion specifically warranted such a lax gesture.

At the same time, she could not forget the last few months of their association. She had been most concerned over Baxter's increasing melancholy, to the point where she had begun to worry that he was seriously ill. Looking at him now, however, she realized she had never seen him look so well.

His square-cut face seemed to glow with an inner excitement she had never perceived in him before. The shoulders that had seemed to bow with the weight of an unspoken anguish were now held erect, seemingly adding height and power to his sturdy form.

Even his eyes, which had once looked as bleak as a gray wintry sky, actually appeared to sparkle, as if they were hiding a delicious secret known only to him. Much as she hated to admit it, the change of occupation had done him the world of good.

He inclined his head as she continued to stare at him. "It's good to see you again, Cecily."

As always, the use of her Christian name gave her a small start. Her hand fluttered at her throat, and she snatched it down. "And you, Baxter. What brings you back to the hotel, today?" Carefully leaving the door open, she advanced into the room.

"I happened to be passing by and thought I would drop in to pay my respects."

Disappointed that he had acted merely on impulse, Cecily inwardly chided herself. "I'm so glad you did. It's always a pleasure to see you." She moved over to the table and took her usual seat at the head of it. "Won't you sit down?"

The invitation was routine, offered without conscious thought. To her astonishment, Baxter took a seat facing the bookshelves. Never once had he ever sat down in the library with her, in spite of her repeated requests that he do so.

Cecily cleared her throat and hoped her voice would not betray her disquiet. "Do you . . . still have those wonderful little cigars you always carried?"

He raised an eloquent eyebrow. "Do you still indulge in that unfortunate habit? I was rather hoping that you would have forsaken smoking cigars once the source was no longer readily available." He frowned, his cool gaze raking her face. "Unless you have acquired another source?"

Cecily sighed. "No, I have to confess I have not smoked a single cigar since you left this establishment. I must also confess that I have missed them sorely."

She watched him withdraw the slim packet from the pocket of his fashionable lounge suit jacket. Perhaps it was the absence of his morning coat that gave him such a casual air, she thought. Yet even without the tails, he managed to convey an aura of quiet elegance.

Taking a cigar from the proffered packet, she waited for him to strike a match. He did so with his usual measured care, though she was gratified to notice that his hand was not quite steady as he cupped the flame and held it to the end of her cigar.

The unfamiliar rush of smoke in her lungs made her cough. It took her a moment or two to regain her breath. "Do forgive me," she said, her voice raspy with the sting of smoke.

Baxter regarded her gravely. "It isn't wise to inhale cigar smoke," he said quietly.

"I don't usually, as you well know." She coughed again and laid the cigar in the silver ashtray in front of her. "As I said, I have not smoked in three months. I am out of practice."

"So I have noticed."

Deciding it was time to change the subject, she asked him, "Have you heard the sad news about Will Jones?"

Baxter's expression altered at once. "Yes, I heard the men talking about it at the George and Dragon. Poor man. How dreadful it must be to die all alone like that."

"I know. I can't seem to stop thinking about it." She picked up the cigar again and tried another experimental puff. This time the fragrant smoke drifted easily from her mouth. Even so, for some reason she found the taste unpleasant.

For once, the sensation of smoking failed to relax her. In fact, she thought, dropping the cigar back into the ashtray, she wondered now how she could ever have enjoyed it so much.

"I plan to attend the funeral, of course," she said when Baxter made no further comment. She hesitated, then asked casually, "When do you plan to return to London?"

"At the week's end. I should be able to attend the funeral as well. I don't suppose there will be too many family members there."

"As far as I know, Will has no family. He does have a good many friends, however."

"He does, indeed. The vicar will miss him, no doubt."

Impatient with this mundane conversation, Cecily asked abruptly, "Are you hungry?"

Baxter looked a little startled. "It has been quite a while since I have eaten, I must confess."

"In that case, would you be interested in joining me for afternoon tea? I find I have missed the midday meal, and I am quite ravenous."

Once more his smile unsettled her. "That would be very

nice, Cecily. Thank you." He stood and moved around to pull back her chair.

Hiding her confusion, she rose, her gaze concentrated on the clock. "I'll have one of the maids bring it up to the conservatory. It will be quieter there than in the dining room."

He didn't answer, and she peeked up at him. Unable to tell from his expression what was on his mind, she asked, "Does that meet with your approval?"

She expected him to move away and allow her to walk around the table. Instead, he stood where he was, with no more than a foot between them.

"That will be most pleasant."

She frowned. "Somehow those words do not carry conviction."

He laughed then, a rare, deep, rich sound that warmed her through. "My apologies. For a moment I assumed that the invitation was for afternoon tea in your suite. I do understand, however, that such an interlude might well compromise your good name. The conservatory will serve very well."

Aware that her mouth had fallen slack, Cecily snapped it shut. Not only his words, but the sudden light in his eyes had shocked her. This was a very changed man indeed. She wasn't certain whether to feel elated about that conviction or cautious about what the transformation might bring about.

Seated with him in the conservatory a few minutes later, she pretended an interest in the salmon paste and cucumber sandwiches while she recovered her composure.

Baxter, to her chagrin, seemed perfectly at ease, apparently unaware of the chaos he was producing in his companion's mind. "I really must say," he murmured, looking about him with obvious pleasure, "this hotel takes on an entirely different ambience when one is the guest instead of the servant."

"I would venture that it is the person, not the surroundings, that is different." Cecily carefully avoided his gaze as she studied the tiered dish of cakes and pastries. Selecting a small square cake with half of a glacé cherry imbedded in its pink icing, she took a bite of the creamy morsel.

"Are you saying that I have changed?" Baxter said, sounding amused.

"I am saying that you have become . . . more relaxed perhaps." She risked a glance at him.

He was watching her with a faint smile hovering around his mouth. "You are uncomfortable with that?"

She shrugged. "Not at all. I am rather surprised, that's all. It intrigues me that your new position has achieved such a metamorphosis. It makes me curious as to what that occupation can be."

Once again his rich laugh rang out. "It is not in the least controversial, if that is what you are concerned about. I wondered when you were going to ask me about it."

She finished the cake and dabbed at her mouth with the white linen serviette. "I hesitated to bring up the topic, since you seemed disinclined to talk about it."

His smile faded. "I was concerned that the subject might distress you."

"Piffle! Why should it?"

He lifted his hands and let them fall. "I left your employ for another."

"Which you had a perfect right to do."

"And you had no qualms about my decision, I take it."

To her intense discomfort, she felt her cheeks growing warm. "Naturally I was upset. Your work and your advice have been invaluable to me. I was aware of how much I would miss you."

"I missed you, also, Cecily."

For once she was at a loss for words. Dropping her gaze, she contemplated the pastries once more.

"I am the assistant manager of a large bank in Thread-needle Street," Baxter said quietly. He named the bank, and Cecily sharply raised her chin.

"Isn't that the bank that sponsored the women's bicycle club?"

Baxter nodded solemnly. "It is, indeed."

Cecily narrowed her eyes. "You wouldn't have anything to do with that, by any chance?"

"Perhaps." She continued to gaze at him until he sighed and added, "Oh, very well. I recommended the Pennyfoot. An associate of mine at the bank told me about his wife's bicycle club and mentioned they were selecting a place to go for their outing. I told him about St. Bartholomew's Week and the Pennyfoot in particular. His wife liked the idea apparently."

"Thank you, Baxter," Cecily said warmly. "That was very nice of you. As you can imagine, I appreciate the business, even if it meant there was no room for you."

Baxter nodded. "That's why I decided to stay at the George and Dragon. I expected the hotel to be filled."

"Do you like your new job?"

Her question must have taken him by surprise, as he took a while to answer her. "Yes, I do. Very much. There are fresh challenges every day, on a much larger scale than I was used to here at the Pennyfoot. I enjoy the satisfaction of solving the various problems that arise."

She nodded, trying to swallow her resentment.

"I do miss the Pennyfoot, Cecily," Baxter said quietly. "I have spent many happy years here. I felt it was time to move on, that's all."

That's all. How nonchalantly he could say that. How

could he not know that his leaving had left an emptiness inside her that could never be filled?

"Well," she said briskly, "I must say the change has done you good. You look very well, though I must confess I find your new demeanor somewhat unsettling."

She had expected him to smile at that, but he surprised her by studying her gravely for a moment or two. "My manner hasn't changed," he said at last. "What has changed are the circumstances. I no longer work for you, Cecily. Our relationship is on a different footing now."

She didn't quite know what to say to that. She wasn't sure what he meant by those words. Nor was she at all certain that she was comfortable with the "different footing," as he called it. In fact, she couldn't remember ever feeling so confused in her entire life.

The following morning, Cecily was still trying to come to terms with Baxter's visit. He had left her again without mentioning another meeting. She assumed that he intended to simply drop in whenever the mood took him.

She rather hoped she wouldn't be there the next time he paid her a visit. That would take the wind out of his sails. He was taking entirely too much for granted. But then, she had to admit, he always had. Now that his arrogance was directed at her personally, however, she found it aggravating.

When Daisy announced that she had a visitor later that morning, Cecily half expected Baxter to stroll into the library. She wasn't sure if she was disappointed or relieved when her caller turned out to be P.C. Northcott.

After sending for some of his favorite Dundee cake and tea, Cecily asked the constable how she could help him.

"I've come to talk to Colonel Fortescue, ma'am," Northcott said, tipping his helmet back further on head so that he could scratch at his receding hairline. "I always have a bit of trouble when I'm conversing with that gentleman. I wonder if you would mind h'accompanying me when I question him?"

"Not at all." Cecily glanced at the clock. "I should think he's up and about by now. Most likely taking his morning stroll in the rose garden. Why don't we go and look? By the time we return, your tea and cake should have arrived."

"Very good, ma'am. Much obliged, I'm sure." The constable waited for her to precede him out of the door, then kept up a steady chatter while they walked down the hallway to the lobby.

Ned tipped his hat before opening the door with a flourish. "Morning, mum. Morning, Bobby. How's yer mother off for dripping, then?"

Northcott looked down his nose at the young man, obviously declining to waste his breath on such vulgarity.

Ned winked at Cecily and stood back to let them pass. She was about to step over the threshold when Sid Barker appeared in the doorway.

The stiff sea breeze had flung his hair in all directions. Damp, limp strands hung over his face, giving his mournful features even more of a soulful look.

"Jolly windy out there today," he muttered as he slunk by Cecily.

"Too windy for riding a bicycle," Cecily said pleasantly.

Sid wasn't listening, however. After one startled look at P.C. Northcott, he put his head down and scuttled down the hallway.

"Bit of a strange one, that," Ned remarked as Cecily stepped outside.

"It wouldn't do for us all to be the same," Cecily chided briskly.

"No, mum, you're right about that." Ned laughed, a

hollow sound that seemed to echo after them as the constable followed her down the steps.

In spite of the brisk wind blowing straight off the ocean, Cecily spotted the colonel snoozing on his favorite perch, which happened to be a long bench underneath the arbor. He looked so comfortable that she regretted having to stir him.

When she touched his shoulder, he came awake with a jerk. "What? What? Where are the blighters, then? Don't let them take you by surprise! Downright crafty, those bastards . . . always creeping up on you—"

"Colonel," Cecily said quietly, "P.C. Northcott is here. He'd like a word with you."

The colonel blinked, then sat up. "Is he, by Jove? Well send him in, then." He looked around him, as if realizing for the first time that he was outside in the rose garden. "Oh, sorry, old chap. Didn't see you standing there. Dashed sun in my eyes, you know."

"Yes, well . . ." Northcott cleared his throat rather noisily, took out his notebook, and licked the end of his pencil. "Now, then, Colonel, h'if you don't mind, I'd like you to inform me h'exactly what time you vacated this 'ere establishment in order to proceed to the George and Dragon Inn on the night of August 24th."

Fortescue's eyelids began flapping wildly up and down. He sent Cecily a hunted look. "What's he saying?"

"He wants to know what time you left the Pennyfoot on Monday night." Cecily patted the colonel's hand. "The night of the feast, remember?"

The colonel shook his head so hard his teeth rattled. "No, I don't remember, old girl. Never went to any feast. I just had my usual pint with a brandy chaser."

"H'and what time did you depart from here to go down there, then, sir?" Northcott asked, with admirable patience, Cecily thought.

She couldn't imagine why the constable was so interested in the colonel's activities. In any case, it was unlikely that Fortescue had the slightest idea what time he left.

"I left at the usual time, old boy," the colonel said, proving her wrong. He puffed out his chest as if he was proud of that achievement. "Never miss. Half past seven, on the dot."

"I see, sir." The constable scribbled something down. "I understand, Colonel, that it is not your 'abit to wear a watch, h'am I correct?"

"Perfectly correct, old boy. Can't abide the pesky things. Never could. Dashed nuisance, if you want my opinion."

"Then p'raps you wouldn't mind explaining to me, sir, 'ow it is you know precisely what time you left this here hotel on Monday night?"

Fortescue looked nonplussed for a moment, while Cecily wondered just what the constable was getting at.

"My good man," the colonel said pompously, "if you must know, I left the hotel at the sound of the church bells. Been doing that for years. Every night, at the first stroke of those bells, I set off for the pub. Every night I arrive there at a quarter past eight."

He smiled and patted his chest. "Tell the blasted time by me, they can. Just about gives me enough time to down my usual six pints before they call, 'Time, gentleman, please!'"

"I see, sir. In that case, p'raps you can tell me if you saw anything h'unusual on your way down there on Monday night?"

Cecily frowned. Since the colonel always took the path across the Downs, presumably Northcott wanted to know if the gentleman had seen Will on his way to the pub. But if the colonel had started out while the bells were still ringing, he would have been far ahead of Will on the path.

What really concerned Cecily, however, was the reason

behind all these intense questions. They hardly seemed necessary in view of the fact that Will's death was an accident. If Will's death was, indeed, an accident.

Once more she felt the sense of foreboding. Something was very wrong, she could sense it. Something was very wrong, indeed.

CHAPTER

❈ 7 ❈

Samuel whistled as he marched across the yard toward the kitchen door. He was in a particularly good mood that morning. For one thing, the sun had dried out the morning mist, and the balmy breeze felt warm on his face.

He sniffed the fragrant air, enjoying the smell of newly cut grass mingled with the lingering aroma of fried bacon. His stomach churned, and his mouth watered as he thought about the hot Cornish pasty waiting for him on top of the stove.

Every morning about this time Doris put the pasty on the stove to warm up. He wasn't really sure whether it was the thought of that delicious pastry filled with meat, potatoes, and rich gravy or Doris's pert, smiling face that quickened his steps as he neared the kitchen. A little bit of both, he reckoned, and smiled as he pushed the door open.

Doris stood at the sink, as usual, her white apron sweeping the floor as she leaned forward to reach for a plate. The long sleeves of her dress were rolled up above the elbows, and damp tendrils escaped from beneath the ruffled white cap covering her light brown hair.

"Hallo, beautiful," Samuel called out as he closed the door behind him. "Got my pasty ready, have you? I'm ruddy starving, I am."

Doris turned a flushed face toward him. "It's on the stove."

Samuel crossed the kitchen and picked up the pasty, yelping as the hot pastry burned his fingers. Flipping it back and forth between his hands, he carried it over to the kitchen table and dropped it onto the scrubbed surface.

"Where's the babies, then?" he asked, looking around the kitchen. "Out with Daisy, are they?"

Doris nodded and wiped an arm across her forehead. "She took them for a walk down the Esplanade."

Samuel pulled up a chair as close to the sink as he could get, then straddled it, propping his elbows on the back of it. As usual, he'd timed it about right.

Michel was on his break before starting the midday meal, and Mrs. Chubb and the maids were either in the dining room or cleaning the bedrooms. For a few minutes at least, Samuel had Doris all to himself.

"I haven't heard you singing lately," he remarked, knowing full well that the mention of singing to Doris was guaranteed to get her close attention.

"That's because I haven't done any lately." She lifted up a bony arm and examined the dripping plate she held. "I'm going to lose me voice if I don't practice."

"Then why aren't you singing?" Samuel swept an arm in

the air. "Look, there's nobody here now. You could sing to me."

Doris sent him a bashful look over her shoulder. "Why would you want to hear the likes of me singing?"

"Because I think you have a beautiful voice and I really like to hear you sing. You sound like the angels must sound in heaven."

She giggled. "Oh, go on with you. You're just saying that."

"No, I'm not." Samuel drew his thumb across his chest. "Cross me heart."

Doris put the plate on the draining board and reached for another. "Michel doesn't like me singing in the kitchen. He says as how he can't concentrate with all that caterwauling going on."

"Oh, don't take no notice of Michel. Just wait until you're a famous Variety star. Then he'll have to pay to come and hear you. He doesn't know how lucky he is, being able to hear you for free."

Doris's face glowed as she looked at him. "I really am going to be famous one day, Samuel. I know I am."

Gazing at her lovely brown eyes, Samuel said passionately, "I know you are, too. Even madam says as how you've got a marvelous voice. Everybody does."

Doris sighed and turned back to the sink. "I just wish I could go to Wellercombe and audition at the Hippodrome. I know if they heard me, they'd give me a chance."

Samuel fought with his conscience. The last thing in the world he wanted was for Doris to go off to Wellercombe and be in the Variety halls. He had the distinct feeling that once she became a real singer, he'd never see her again. On the other hand, he'd do just about anything to make her happy. "I could take you to Wellercombe," he offered, praying hard that she wouldn't agree.

"Oh, Samuel, that's really nice of you." She gave him a smile that would warm his heart all day long. "I'm not old enough, though," she said disconsolately as she turned back to the sink. "I have to be eighteen before they'll take me on at the Hippodrome."

At least another two years. Samuel offered up a silent prayer of thanks to Whomever might be listening. "Well, in the meantime, you'd better keep singing if you don't want to lose your voice."

He thought about it while Doris swished plates around in the suds. "Tell you what," he said at last, "how about coming over to the stables on your afternoon off? You could sing all you like while I polish the harnesses. That way you could practice, and I could hear you sing."

"Really? I'd like that. I could try out my new songs."

"I'd like to hear them."

She smiled at him again, and his spirits rose even more. Life was really very good to him, he told himself as he took a huge bite out of the pasty.

Munching contentedly, Samuel tried to think of something else that might interest Doris. "I think someone borrowed one of the traps last night," he said when he'd emptied his mouth.

Doris shook the suds off a large serving dish. "What do you mean, borrowed? Took it without asking you, you mean?"

"Yeah." Samuel finished another bite of the pasty. "Don't know who it was. Nobody's supposed to take the traps out without letting me know where they are. I wouldn't have known, except I found some gravel and bits of grass on the seat. I don't know where it could have come from. Anyhow, I know I cleaned them both last night."

"P'raps Mr. Ridlington took one out. He's new, so he might not know all the rules."

"Yeah, p'raps he did. I shall have to tell him that he has to tell me when he takes a trap out." Samuel finished the pasty and wiped his mouth on his sleeve. "That were a bit of all right. Just hit the spot. One thing I have to say, that Mrs. Chubb knows how to make good pastry."

"Don't tell Michel that," Doris said, looking nervously over her shoulder. "He hates us saying anything about Mrs. Chubb's cooking."

"Michel doesn't frighten me." Samuel pushed his chair back and got reluctantly to his feet. "Anyhow, I have to get back to the stables now. I have to clean that trap again. Don't forget what I said, now. Come over to the stables on your afternoon off, and I'll listen to you sing, all right?"

Doris nodded. "All right. I'll come."

Whistling, Samuel crossed the yard again, his hands in his pockets, his head in the air. Now that he had something good to look forward to, the bright summer morning seemed even more enjoyable.

Inside the hotel Mrs. Chubb was not finding the morning quite so delightful. Primrose Parsons, the tall, gaunt president of the women's bicycle club, had cornered the housekeeper in the hallway outside the dining room and was loudly complaining about the service in the hotel.

"I had to wait twenty minutes for my crumpets," she said, her deep voice booming down the corridor like the foghorn on the new lighthouse. "Absolutely disgraceful. By the time I got them, they were cold. Really! I expected much better service than this, considering the outrageous price of the rooms."

Mrs. Chubb cast an apprehensive glance over her shoulder. It wouldn't do for one of the guests to hear this unpleasant woman. Or worse, Mr. Ridlington or madam.

Shuddering at the thought, Mrs. Chubb managed a smile,

even though her resentment smoldered inside. "I'm very sorry you were inconvenienced, ma'am. I assure you, it won't happen again."

Primrose Parsons sniffed, her long nose quivering like an inquisitive hedgehog. "That's as may be. Promises are not going to cure my indigestion, however. Kindly have a digestive powder sent up to my room at once. I shall have to lie down until this terrible pain subsides."

"Of course, ma'am. Right away." In a hurry now to be rid of the pesky woman, the housekeeper dropped a curtsey and tried to escape from her corner.

"Please send up a tray of fresh warm scones and a pot of tea. And don't forget the Devonshire cream and strawberry jam."

"Yes, ma'am." The silly woman was going to end up with worse indigestion than she had now, Mrs. Chubb thought, wishing she could tell the old bat what she really thought of her. That's if she really did have indigestion.

Anyone who ate the way Primrose Parsons did deserved to have a stomachache. Although it was Mrs. Chubb's considered opinion that Miss Parsons's stomach was stronger than anyone else's in the entire hotel.

To her vast relief, the woman moved out of the way, allowing the housekeeper to edge past her and hurry down the hallway to the lobby.

Rushing down the stairs to the kitchen, Mrs. Chubb thought longingly of Ethel. If only madam could find the money to hire her back. It would be such a blessing to have another pair of hands, especially when they were as experienced as Ethel's.

Making up her mind to mention it to madam at the first opportunity, Mrs. Chubb threw open the kitchen door and charged once more into the fray.

*   *   *

Accompanying the constable back to the hotel, Cecily paid scant attention to his idle chatter about the topiary, which John the gardener kept trimmed with loving care. The ornate shapes of peacocks, coaxed into shape from the thick laurel bushes lining the croquet lawn, were quite spectacular, and normally she would have enjoyed the constable's effusive praise.

This morning, however, her mind was on the policeman's questions put to the colonel. She couldn't escape the uneasy feeling that there was a purpose behind Northcott's interest in the eccentric gentleman.

Determined to learn just what that purpose was, Cecily mulled over her opening question. P.C. Northcott had to be handled carefully, or he would close up tighter than the lid of a snuffbox. On the other hand, if she played her cards right, he would tell her everything he knew.

Deliberately she slowed her step, forcing the constable to drop back as well, something he was loathe to do, she could tell. He was anxious to get back to the library and his Dundee cake.

"Such a tragedy, that unfortunate accident," she began, pretending to be interested in the game of croquet taking place on the lawn. She paused for a moment to watch, causing the constable to huff impatiently as he came to a halt at her side.

"Yes, ma'am, indeed it were," he said, puffing out his chest.

They both watched in silence as a young woman in a long gray skirt hit the wooden ball with a resounding smack of her mallet, sending it rolling forward toward the iron hoop planted in the ground. The woman bobbed up and down in delight as the ball rolled through the wicket.

After a moment or two, Cecily moved off again, in the

direction of the hotel steps. "It seems such a strange thing to happen," she murmured. "I mean, Will Jones has walked that path every night since I can remember. According to Phoebe, he seemed perfectly well when she saw him that afternoon. Yet on the way home he strayed close enough to the cliff's edge to lose his footing and plunge to his death."

Watching the constable out of the corner of her eye, her pulse quickened when she saw him jerk his head around to stare at her.

"It does seem strange, yes, ma'am. I agree with you there."

She could hear it in his voice—a wary hesitancy that told her he knew much more than he wanted to tell her. Deciding to wait until they were in the library before probing further, Cecily quickened her step. The constable happily hurried along with her, almost to the point of running by the time they reached the steps.

Once inside the library, Cecily waited until Northcott had consumed most of the cake, then said airily, "I suppose if Will's death hadn't been an accident, the police would know it by now. After all, nothing much escapes our local constabulary these days, am I right?"

"Quite right, Mrs. Sinclair." The constable sat back in his chair and beamed at her. "We pride ourselves on being the best in the country."

"And I'm sure it is well deserved." Cecily nodded, as if to reassure herself. "That's why I am quite sure poor Will simply missed his footing and fell."

There was a short pause while she held her breath. Then Northcott said cautiously, "I'm not supposed to say anything until we've done a proper h'investigation, but I don't suppose there's any harm in telling you, Mrs. Sinclair— though you have to promise me, on your word of honor, that you will not breathe a word of this to anyone else."

She might have known he wouldn't be able to contain himself for long. Her apprehension increased as she murmured, "Why, constable, how could you think I would indulge such a confidence?"

Northcott nodded, looking uncomfortable. "Oh, I know you wouldn't, ma'am. It's just that I 'ave to caution you, like. It's me job."

"Quite. Consider me cautioned." That didn't mean she'd promised him anything, she silently added, trying to salve her conscience. It was imperative now that she learn what he knew.

"Well," the constable said, leaning forward with a conspiratorial whisper, "not that I want to blow me own trumpet, like, but I was the very first person to suspect that Will's death was not h'an h'accident after all."

So her premonition had been right. Cecily opened her eyes wide. "Really?" she said in a breathless whisper. "However did you find that out?"

Northcott sat back in his chair and puffed out his chest. "Simple deduction, that's what. If I say so meself. I happened to get a visit from Bernard Willoughby, the blind man what lives in one of those little cottages overlooking the harbor."

"Oh, yes, I know Mr. Willoughby. He's always walking his black labrador along the beach." Cecily smiled. "No matter what the weather, the two of them are out there every day, summer and winter alike."

Northcott nodded. "That'd be the chap. Anyhow, he was on the south side of the cliffs, which is the dry side of the bay." He paused, as if he'd told Cecily something she didn't already know.

Cecily tried to curb her impatience. "That's where he usually walks at night. I think the dog takes him there, actually, and brings him back."

"I wouldn't be at all surprised." Once more the constable paused maddeningly. "Anyhow, he was out walking on the beach the evening of August 24th, which was the night Will died. He said as how he heard a loud splash, as if something heavy had fallen into the sea."

"Oh, my!" Cecily exclaimed.

Northcott looked pleased with her reaction. "Of course, being blind, like, Bernard couldn't be sure of the time. But he thinks it were round about the time Will would be walking home."

"He thinks he heard Will fall down the cliff?"

"Yes, ma'am. That's what he reckons. He heard something else and all." Northcott preened himself. "Bernard says as how he heard footsteps after the splash. His dog whined, and Bernard called out, asking if anyone were there."

The constable paused for effect. "No one answered him, Mrs. Sinclair. No one at all. He didn't think much about it after that, until the next morning when he heard about Will's death from the milkman. That's when Bernard came to tell me."

"It could have been someone else throwing something away," Cecily pointed out. "Unfortunately some people seem to have no compunction about throwing their discards into the sea. You'd be surprised what turns up on the beach during a storm."

"I don't think it were anyone else, ma'am, begging your pardon. I think that what Bernard heard was Will's body hitting the water."

"Did he hear Will cry out?"

Northcott looked taken aback. "Not that I know of. All he mentioned hearing was the footsteps and his dog whining."

"But if Bernard heard footsteps . . ." Cecily prompted, already way ahead of him.

"That meant that someone else was up there when Will fell in."

"I see," Cecily said, allowing a note of doubt to creep into her voice. She could tell by his expression that he was holding something back, and she wanted to know what it was. "So you think someone pushed Will over the cliff?"

"Not think, ma'am. I know. See, when I talked to Bernard, right away I thought something sounded fishy. So I called Dr. Prestwick and had him do a postmortem on the body."

Her interest well and truly caught now, Cecily leaned forward, her gaze intent on the policeman's ruddy face. "Do tell me, Constable. What did the doctor find?"

"He found something very suspicious, that's what," Northcott said, sounding smug. "Something very suspicious, indeed. Just as I expected."

Cecily waved an impatient hand. "Yes, but what did he find?"

"Ah, well, I'm afraid I'm not at liberty to divulge that." To Cecily's intense disappointment, Northcott placed his cup and saucer on the hearth and rose awkwardly to his feet. "I've said too much already, if I'm not mistaken. Thank you for the tea and the cake, Mrs. Sinclair. Much obliged. Please give my regards to Mrs. Chubb and tell her that her cooking gets better every time I taste it."

"I'll be sure to pass that along," Cecily promised.

She walked with Northcott to the lobby, where Ned was waiting to open the door for him. She knew it would be useless to ask the constable any more questions. He had already told her more than he was supposed to divulge and was no doubt at this very moment regretting that he'd been so expansive.

Her assumption was proved correct when Northcott leaned toward her at the door and muttered quietly so that

Ned couldn't hear, "You won't forget, Mrs. Sinclair, that this little matter is strictly between you and me. Just keep it under your hat."

"I won't forget," Cecily assured him.

Northcott nodded, lifted his helmet, then trudged down the steps as if reluctant to leave.

Cecily turned back to the lobby, her mind already working on her next step. She was shaken, however, when she saw Ned's expression. He was staring after the policeman with what she could only describe as sheer hatred in his eyes. For a moment he wore a positively evil look on his face. Then he must have realized she'd noticed his intense scowl.

The next instant his smile had wiped off all trace of the anger that had seemed to consume him. The transformation was so swift and so complete that Cecily almost thought she'd imagined that foul expression.

"Looks like a beautiful day out there, Mrs. S," Ned exclaimed with a wide grin. "I might take a butchers at the beach beauties later on. Makes me heart pound it does, seeing all them ladies in their bathing costumes."

He held his hand over his heart with a comical look on his face, but Cecily didn't feel much like laughing. She left him at the door, her mind still visualizing quite another kind of look on her doorman's face.

It was quite plain to see that Ned bore a very strong grudge against P.C. Northcott. Yet as far as she knew, they had never met each other before today.

Perhaps she had imagined it after all, she told herself as she climbed the stairs to her suite. Perhaps it was merely a trick of the light that made Ned's eyes gleam with such loathing.

Nevertheless, she promised herself that she would watch

that young man closely, and at the slightest sign of trouble, she would get rid of him.

If only Baxter were still working for her. He would know how to handle the matter. No doubt Malcolm would, too. But somehow she was reluctant to discuss her fears with Malcolm Ridlington. He wouldn't understand. She wasn't even sure she did.

One thing she did know. From what she had heard from P.C. Northcott, it seemed that someone could have been on the cliffs with Will that night. But if someone had pushed Will over, why hadn't he cried out?

There was one person who might be able to help her with that question, and she decided she would pay Dr. Prestwick a visit that very afternoon.

CHAPTER

8

"Ladies, please! Kindly remember that this is a place of worship and should be treated with respect." Phoebe glared at the group of girls who stood huddled together in front of the pulpit. As usual, the dreadful creatures were giggling and carrying on as if they were in a school playground instead of young ladies assembled in a house of God.

Phoebe fanned herself with her lace-edged handkerchief. To make matters worse, Algie was working in the vestry, within earshot of her dance troupe. At the slightest provocation, he was likely to make a fuss. She had quite enough trouble as it was, without having to put up with his petty complaints.

"Why do we have to rehearse in here?" a tall, lanky girl asked loudly. "Why can't we do it outside?"

"Because, Dora," Phoebe said, mustering what little patience she had left, "as I've already stated, it is raining outside. I really don't think you want to prance around the church in the pouring rain, now do you?"

"Well, why can't we rehearse in the church hall, then?" a hefty, dark-haired girl demanded.

"Yeah, why can't we?" the rest of the girls chorused.

"Because," Phoebe said firmly, "Miss Pengrath is in there setting up for the flower show on Saturday. Please stop complaining and let us proceed with the rehearsal. The clipping is tomorrow, and in spite of all the rehearsing, none of you seem to know what you are doing." With admirable restraint she refrained from adding that their incompetence was the normal state of affairs.

"There's not enough room to rehearse in here," Dora grumbled. "Marion's taking up all the room there is."

"'Ere, watch it!" The dark-haired girl jammed an elbow into Dora's side. "You saying I'm flipping fat?"

Dora looked her up and down. "Nah, not fat. Just big, that's all. Like a blinking whale."

For answer, Marion took a handful of stringy blond hair and tugged. Dora yelled while the rest of the girls, sensing a fight, nudged each other and giggled.

"Go on, sock 'er one," one of them urged.

"Ladies!" Phoebe screeched, reflecting that the term seemed wholly unsuitable for such reprehensible trouble-makers. "I simply will not tolerate such disgraceful behavior. Anyone who does not wish to participate in this event is free to leave. Right now. This very instant."

Marion tossed her head and began to march down the aisle. One by one the girls fell in behind her, until no one was left in front of the pulpit.

Enraged, Phoebe dashed up the opposite aisle with

remarkable agility. Reaching the door ahead of the girls, she held up her hand.

Marion stopped abruptly in front of her, and the girls each bumped into the one in front before coming to a staggering halt. They stood, watching expectantly and with glee on their faces while Phoebe struggled to contain her fury.

In a strangled voice, she pronounced each word carefully. "As I said, you are free to leave. If you wish to continue performing in my presentations, however, I strongly suggest you return to the front of the church and continue with this miserable rehearsal. Otherwise, I shall see that your performing days are over. Permanently."

"Well, cor blimey, Mrs. Carter-Holmes," Marion said in an injured tone, "why didn't you flipping say so in the first place?" Turning, she marched back down the aisle and took up her position in front of the pulpit again.

The rest of the group filed down, giggling amongst themselves, then finally arranged themselves alongside Marion. All except Dora, who stood at the end of the front pew with her arms folded.

"I'm not dancing with that overgrown elephant, so there. She's always standing on me flipping feet. I'll be a blinking cripple if I dance with her again."

Gritting her teeth, Phoebe advanced on the belligerent girl. "You either dance with Marion or not at all."

Dora puffed out her breath, then muttered, "Oh, all right. Just keep her out of me way, that's all."

"Don't you worry, droopy drawers, I'll stay out of your way," Marion muttered.

"Now, ladies," Phoebe called out, doing her level best to ignore the sparring opponents, "as you all know, you will each be responsible for twelve people. Since there are eight of you, that will mean you will lead almost a hundred people in the dancing. It will take that many to completely join hands around the church."

"Seems a stupid waste of time, if you ask me," someone muttered, loud enough for Phoebe to hear.

Personally, she rather agreed with the child, but Algie had insisted on the ceremony. All she could hope was that it wouldn't rain on Friday. Heaven only knew what she would do if it poured again.

It had been difficult enough persuading everyone to join in the ceremony. If it hadn't been for Cecily's bicycle club members, she would never have found enough people in time. As it was, everyone, with the exception of the club president, that haughty Miss Parsons, and that strange fellow, Sid Barker, had accepted her invitation.

She would have liked to have included the new manager of the Pennyfoot, Malcolm Ridlington, but he had also declined, stating that he would be too busy to attend the ceremony.

Actually Phoebe wasn't too disappointed by his decision. After talking to him briefly, she had formed a distinctly unfavorable opinion of the man.

"Mrs. Carter-Holmes, Isabelle's not in her place," Dora said loudly.

Gathering her thoughts, Phoebe looked over to where Isabelle stood admiring the Helmsboro chalice. "Isabelle? Get back in line at once, child. You have all wasted enough time as it is."

"I was just looking at the cup," Isabelle muttered as she wandered back to the line. "It's so pretty. Isn't that what it's for? To look at it?"

"Yes, indeed it is," Phoebe agreed. "But the time to admire it is at the ceremony on Friday. Not now."

"We'll be bleeding dancing around the church at the

ceremony," Marion whined. "How are we going to look at it then?"

"*After* you have finished dancing, of course. You will all stay for the service that Algie will conduct." She clasped her hands and looked around her at the rows of empty pews. "It will be so wonderful to have the church filled to capacity. It will be the first time since Dr. McDuff's funeral."

"Oh, me Gawd, I hope we don't get any surprises like that one on Friday," Marion said, nudging Isabelle in the ribs. "Remember when they opened the coffin and it weren't the doctor inside? I thought I was going to spew me innards all over the people in front of me, I did."

Isabelle put her hand over her mouth. "Eeyew, Marion."

The rest of the group immediately and loudly uttered cries of disgust.

"Tell her to shut up, Mrs. Carter-Holmes," Dora demanded. "She's making me blinking ill."

"I've only got to look at you, and I get ill," Marion said rudely.

"You will all be very ill indeed if you don't pay attention!" Phoebe bellowed. "Now, please get in line to rehearse the dance steps."

The girls shuffled obediently into a ragged line.

Phoebe pulled a deep breath to calm her nerves. "Now, remember you will each be leading twelve people in the dance, as well as singing the song we rehearsed."

She proceeded to show them the steps once more, her dainty feet executing the simple movements with expert precision. "Like so . . . one, two, three . . . one, two, three . . . one, two, three, and four."

She looked up, mollified to see the girls watching her with avid attention. "Now, all of you do it with me. One, two, three . . . one, two, th—"

A shrill scream echoed eerily throughout the rafters. "Get your big fat foot off my toe, you blithering idiot!" Dora howled.

"I wasn't on your flipping toe," Marion yelled back. "It was Isabelle. She's got bigger feet than I have."

"Oo, I have not," Isabelle wailed. "You're shoes are as big as boats. My dad says as how he can see your feet coming around the corner before the rest of you gets there."

Raucous laughter greeted this statement.

Phoebe jumped up and down, flapping her hands in a futile attempt to restore order. "Ladies, ladies, if you *please!*"

The door of the vestry flew open, and Algie emerged, his face as red as a ripe tomato. Phoebe saw him mouth something, but the noise was so bad that she failed to hear the words.

Annoyed that her son had witnessed her inability to maintain control of the situation, Phoebe found that her temper finally snapped. Reaching out, she hauled on the arm of the nearest girl. It happened to be Dora, who was on the verge of hysterics, it seemed.

In Phoebe's opinion there was only one way to deal with hysterics. Lifting her gloved hand, she gave the girl a light slap on the face.

Silence was restored almost at once. Dora looked at her, her eyes wide with shock, one hand holding her cheek. "You flipping hit me," she said in disbelief.

Murmurs of oohs and aahs drifted from the other girls' open mouths. Even Algie looked taken aback at this affront.

"I did not hit you," Phoebe said tightly. "I merely tapped your cheek. You were in great danger of becoming hysterical, and that would have been extremely harmful to you. We might even have been obliged to call in the doctor."

"I bleeding wish," Marion muttered. "Bit of all right, that Dr. Prestwick."

"He wouldn't look twice at you," someone else said. She was immediately shushed by several of the girls as Phoebe glared.

"What I did, Dora," Phoebe continued, "was merely to attempt to bring you out of your fit, and it seems as if I succeeded. You should be immensely grateful to me. I have saved you from a nasty experience."

Dora stared at her for a moment, then lowered her hand. "Thank you, Mrs. Carter-Holmes," she said doubtfully.

Immensely relieved, Phoebe glanced at the rest of the girls to see how well she had convinced them of her good intentions. Isabelle, it seemed, had once more wandered away.

Phoebe's gazed moved to the pedestal, and her heart stopped. Isabelle was in the act of lifting the cumbersome case from its perch.

"No!" Phoebe screamed. "Don't touch that!"

Isabelle jumped, and, as Phoebe watched helplessly, the glass case began to slip from the girl's fragile grasp.

She would never know from where Algie sprung. One minute Phoebe was staring imminent disaster full in the face, and the next, her son had made a spectacular dive and somehow caught the case before it hit the floor, where it surely would have shattered into a million pieces.

Unable to believe that Algie had managed such an impossible feat, Phoebe sank onto the nearest pew, certain that any minute she would faint dead away.

The girls were silent as Algie hoisted the case back onto its perch. Isabelle inched her way behind Marion's massive bulk, where she was effectively hidden from Phoebe's baleful eye.

Phoebe rose to her feet. In a voice that threatened certain

dismissal if interrupted, she told them, "If that chalice had been damaged in any way, the entire village would be paying for it for the next century. Including every one of you."

Encouraged by the shocked gasps, she added, "In fact, you would all have to pay twice the amount of everyone else's contribution."

"Oo, 'eck," Marion muttered. "That'd put a hole in me dowry, that's for sure."

"You're going to need more than a flipping dowry to get a man to marry you," Dora said scornfully.

Phoebe silenced the troublemakers with a lethal glare. "Now listen to me, all of you. No one, and I repeat no one, will go anywhere near that cup again. And if one more person disrupts this rehearsal in any way, shape, or form, I shall be forced to impose a most severe penalty."

She paused, running her eye over each and every girl until all cringed. "I promise you, you will not care to suffer that way. I trust I make myself clear?"

A subdued chorus of voices chanted, "Yes, Mrs. Carter-Holmes."

"Very well. Now, if it's not too much to ask, we will run through the steps again. In your places, ladies, please."

Thankful that she had the group under control again, Phoebe glanced at Algie for approval. As usual, he was staring at the chalice as if he expected it to grow wings and fly off to heaven.

Irritated that the relic attracted more attention than she'd managed to get from Algie in a lifetime, she was about to turn away when the vicar spun around to face her. The horrified expression on his face shocked her.

"Dora, you should know the steps well enough by now," she said without taking her eyes from her son's face. "Please be so good as to lead the girls around the pews, each of you holding hands, and for goodness sake, try to get the words of the song right."

She waited just long enough to see them start off, then she hurried over to Algie. "Whatever is ailing you?" she demanded urgently. "You look quite pale. Did you hurt yourself when you lifted that chalice back onto the pedestal? I know it's dreadfully heavy. I should have helped you."

The girls were all singing lustily as they skipped down the outside aisle. Phoebe barely noticed. Her attention was concentrated on Algie, who looked as if he might faint dead away.

He cast an agitated glance at the trilling songsters, then shook his head. "I'm . . . quite all right," he muttered. "I have to g-get back to the vestry . . . ah . . . lots of p-paperwork, you know . . ." He nervously readjusted his spectacles, then hurried back to the vestry.

Phoebe watched him go, a frown on her face. Something was apparently troubling him. It was just as obvious that he did not wish to discuss it in front of the dance troupe.

Not that she could blame him. The noise was awful. Someone, it seemed, was dreadfully out of tune and at least two of the girls were giggling instead of singing.

Phoebe tried to put Algie out of her mind as she grilled the girls over and over again, until they at least looked as if they might get it right.

"Practice on your own," she ordered as they trudged wearily out of the church an hour later. "Don't forget to be here bright and early on Friday morning. It will take a little while to get everyone circled around the church. Wait for my signal, Dora, before leading everyone off, please."

Dora nodded, looking glum. "I just hope I hear it," she muttered.

"You'll hear it," Phoebe promised her grimly. "I'll make quite sure of that." She could hardly wait to close the door behind the last girl before hurrying back to the vestry to confront Algie.

The vicar was seated at the desk when she went in, a faraway look in his eyes as he gazed at the narrow strip of leaded glass that served as a window.

"Algie," Phoebe said sharply. "You must tell me what is wrong."

He started, as if he was unaware of her presence until then. Carefully he laid down the pen he held in his trembling fingers. "I don't know how it could have happened," he said, looking at her so desperately that she became quite alarmed.

"How what could have happened?"

"The chalice." He lifted a beseeching hand then let it drop, staring down at it in abject despair.

"Oh, that." Phoebe fanned her face with her handkerchief. "Yes, I must confess, it gave me quite a turn to see that case slipping out of Isabelle's hands. Silly girl. I warned her not to go near it."

She smiled down at Algie in an attempt to cheer him up. "I must say, though, I was most impressed with the way you lunged for the case. I don't think I have ever seen you move quite so fast. Your dexterity really amazed me. Thank heavens you managed to catch it. Just think—"

She stopped short and peered more closely at Algie. His lips were moving, but nothing was coming out. Quite frightened now, she said fiercely, "Algie, you must tell me what is wrong with you. I really don't—"

"It's not the same one," Algie said in a funny little voice that sounded like the plaintive mew of a kitten.

"What's not the same one?" Really, she thought, there were times when she did not understand her son at all.

Algie shook his head, as if he had trouble believing his own muttered words. "The chalice. It's not the same one."

"Not the same one," Phoebe echoed in astonishment. "Whatever do you mean?"

Algie gave her a look of desperation. "I should know. I helped the b-bishop lift it up onto the pedestal. It was so heavy I could . . . ah . . . hardly move it. Now the case is much lighter. I thought at first the ch-chalice wasn't in it."

Phoebe stared at him in growing dismay. "Nonsense," she said tersely after a moment of silence. "Of course it has to be the same chalice. The bishop locked it up inside the case. It's still locked, isn't it?"

Algie nodded, his face steeped in misery.

"Well, then, how could it be a different chalice? It must have been the shock that made you think it wasn't heavy, that's all. I've heard it said that people have extra energy when under stress."

"It wasn't . . . ah . . . stress, Mother," Algie said quietly. "I'm telling you that this is a different c-cup. It looks the same as the other one, but it isn't. It has a d-dent in one side of it. It must have happened when the . . . ah . . . case fell."

Phoebe clutched her throat. "Oh, my. Does it show?"

"Of course it shows. The real ch-chalice is made of pewter an inch thick. It would never . . . ah . . . dent like that, unless someone took a sledgehammer to it. This one looks as if it's made of t-tin."

"Tin?" Phoebe squeaked.

"Tin," Algie said miserably. "Someone has stolen the real chalice, Mother, and left a f-fake in its place."

CHAPTER

❈9❈

Cecily paused in front of her dresser and examined her image with a critical eye. She wore a new frock, something quite different from her usual attire, and she wasn't entirely certain that it suited her somewhat pallid complexion.

Fashioned of fine lawn in a pale champagne, the skirt fell in slim folds to brush the buttons of her cream shoes. Three rows of tucks around the hem matched the narrow tucks down the length of the bodice, which was accented by a row of tiny pearl buttons from her throat to the base of the yoke below her waist.

A band of Swiss eyelet embroidery encircled the Gibson collar and was repeated in a band running down the length of the narrow sleeves, ending in a tiny frill at the cuffs.

She had completed the ensemble with a wide hat of pale

straw, tastefully decorated with a large cream bow of satin ribbon. Her cream gloves were elbow length, fastened with matching pearl buttons.

Cecily frowned in the mirror, wondering if perhaps the frock was too young for her. Sheer impulse had made her buy it. She had seen it displayed in the window of the boutique in the High Street and fell in love with it on sight. Looking at it now, however, she had to admit it had looked better on the scrawny model in the window than it did on her.

She was tempted to change into something more familiar, and might have done so if Gertie hadn't chosen that moment to tap on her door.

The housemaid's eyes widened when she saw Cecily. "Oh, you do look ever so blooming lovely, mum. I never saw you look so nice."

Cecily smiled and thanked the young woman. "You had a message for me? I was just on my way out."

Gertie's bemused expression changed to concern. "Oh, you can't, mum. *He's* here."

Cecily frowned. "Who is here?"

"Mr. Baxter, mum." She grinned and jerked her head in the direction of the stairs. "He's waiting for you in the lobby. I told him as how I'd fetch you down right away."

Cecily hoped her flutter of nerves had not been noticed by the sharp-eyed housemaid. Part of her wished she had made her escape before Baxter had arrived. It really was annoying the way he took her for granted. She couldn't help wondering, though, if her decision to wear the new dress had been prompted by the possibility that Baxter would see her in it.

"Thank you, Gertie," she said, trying to sound indifferent. "Please tell Mr. Baxter I will be down in a few minutes."

"Yes, mum." Gertie started to leave, then paused to give

Cecily a knowing look. "Shall I ask him to wait in the library, mum?"

"I think that would be a good idea, Gertie."

"Yes, mum. So do I." She sped down the corridor as if she could hardly wait to tell him.

Cecily closed the door, then rushed back to the dresser to take another look at the dress. Now that she had no time at all to change, she wished heartily that she'd chosen something else to wear. Something she felt more comfortable wearing. Something a little less . . . frivolous.

She fussed with her hat for a few minutes and turned this way and that in an attempt to view the dress from all angles. Finally, when she could dally no longer, she anxiously headed for the door.

By the time she reached the library she was quite out of breath, although she had taken her time descending the stairs. Longing for the days when she felt entirely relaxed in Baxter's company, she pushed open the door and went in.

This time he stood in front of James's portrait at the fireplace, an unusually grave expression on his face as he gazed up at it.

Cecily would have given a great deal to know what was on his mind, but then he looked at her, and she forgot everything but the changed expression in his eyes.

He studied her in silence for a long moment, while she listened to her own heartbeat. Then he said quietly, "I don't think I have ever seen you look so becoming, Cecily. I trust I'm not taking you away from something special?"

She shook her head. "Not at all, Baxter. I was on my way to see Dr. Prestwick, but that can wait. I am always happy to make time for you."

At the mention of the doctor's name, it was if a curtain had dropped over Baxter's face. Remembering how much he had always disapproved of her friendship with Dr.

Prestwick, Cecily wished she had been just a little more prudent about disclosing her plans.

Regretting having spoilt his moment of admiration, she gestured to a seat at the table. "Won't you sit down? I could have a pot of tea sent up if you wish."

"Thank you, no. I hadn't planned to stay long. I don't want to keep you from your appointment."

He'd sounded like the old Baxter, stiff and formal. She realized then how much she had been enjoying the more recent version of her ex-manager.

"I don't have an appointment," she said gently. "I needed to ask him some questions, that's all. I need to know more about Will's death."

Baxter raised an eyebrow. "Will Jones?"

"Yes." Again she gestured at the chair. "Please sit down, Baxter, and I'll tell you all about it."

He looked at her a moment longer, then gave a brief nod and reached for a chair. Pulling it back, he held it for her while she seated herself. Then he sat down on the opposite side of the table.

"Will's death wasn't an accident," she said, coming straight to the point. "P.C. Northcott told me this morning. He questioned Colonel Fortescue, who would have walked along the path across the Downs the same evening."

"I imagine that was a waste of time," Baxter observed dryly.

"Yes, I suppose it was."

"Northcott believes someone pushed Will over the cliff? That sounds a bit far-fetched. Who would want to kill a penniless old man?"

"That's what I don't understand." Cecily was tempted to ask for a cigar but, remembering her experience with the last one, decided against it. "Apparently Bernard Willoughby heard him fall. Or at least he thinks it was Will's body falling into the ocean. He told the constable he heard footsteps after the splash."

"So you are on the trail of yet another murderer. Is that it?"

She smiled ruefully at him. "I suppose I am." She waited for the usual dire warnings and advice. When none was forthcoming, she felt somewhat deflated. "What intrigues me," she said after a moment or two of silence, "is that apparently Bernard didn't hear Will cry out. I would think that if Will had been pushed over the cliff and fallen to his death, he would have made some kind of noise."

"One would think so," Baxter agreed. "Unless he was already dead when he fell."

"The same thought occurred to me. That's why I want to talk to the doctor. P.C. Northcott told me that Kevin Prestwick had found something very suspicious, but he wouldn't say what it was."

"And you, of course, must discover what it is."

"If someone did indeed deliberately take an innocent man's life for no reason, I want very much to see that person apprehended."

"Indubitably."

She stared at him in vexation. Where were his admonitions about interfering in police business? Where was his concern for her safety? Why didn't he offer to help her, in order to keep her from harm?

Belatedly she remembered the words he'd said shortly before he'd announced that he was leaving his position at the Pennyfoot. Referring to the promise he'd given her late husband on his deathbed, Baxter had implied that he was no longer obligated to protect her.

He had also added that his concern for her well-being had stemmed from a personal interest in her welfare. Could it be that now he was no longer under her employ, he no longer felt concerned for her safety? Had she been mistaken about the reason for his recent visits?

If so, she was left to wonder just what were the reasons behind his casual calls on the Pennyfoot hotel. Perhaps, she thought with an acute sense of disappointment, he was merely curious about his successor.

If so, she would satisfy his curiosity at once. Rising abruptly, she announced, "I think it would be a good idea if you meet Malcolm Ridlington. He appears to be having a great deal of trouble balancing the accounts. Perhaps you can answer some of his questions, if you can spare the time?"

Taken by surprise, Baxter sprang immediately to his feet. "Of course, I will be happy to offer whatever assistance I can. I would not wish to keep you from your mission, however."

Sensing a hint of irony behind his words, Cecily lifted her chin. "My mission, as you call it, can wait, as I've already told you. I will be only too happy to relieve my new manager of his problems. He has been quite irritated by them."

Baxter raised his eyebrows. "I had no idea I'd left the bookkeeping in such a sorry state."

"You didn't," Cecily admitted. "I'm afraid I am not as adept as you were at keeping the figures straight. I let them get into quite a muddle before I hired Mr. Ridlington."

Understanding dawned in his eyes, and he slowly nodded. "Ah, I see. Exactly how long has Mr. Ridlington been working for the Pennyfoot?"

Avoiding his intent gaze, Cecily headed for the door. "Just a few days, actually."

Baxter moved swiftly, reaching the door ahead of her. Pausing before opening it, he murmured, "You waited rather a long time before hiring another manager."

Determined not to let him know the reason she had waited, Cecily shrugged. "I was attempting to do without one. With the added business we've had this summer, I was hoping to hire another maid or two. Unfortunately my bookkeeping skills leave a lot to be desired."

"I see," he murmured, looking just a little disappointed. "I was rather hoping that you had found it difficult to replace me."

"Not at all, Baxter," Cecily said airily. "I had no trouble at all in replacing you." She swept through the door which he had opened, her grand exit somewhat marred by his cynical expression as he followed her.

Malcolm Ridlington looked none too pleased when Cecily introduced her visitor. In fact, he gave Baxter a scathing look that reflected his poor opinion of the Pennyfoot's previous manager.

Baxter, too, looked as if he would like to take hold of the man and run him straight out of the door. When Cecily suggested that Baxter could answer any questions that Malcolm might have, the manager looked most affronted.

"I am perfectly capable of sorting out this mess on my own, Mrs. Sinclair, thank you very much. There is no need to trouble this . . . gentleman any further."

His hesitation before the word *gentleman* was not wasted on Baxter. He inclined his head just a fraction. "I can see that to attempt to assist you would be a waste of valuable time. Therefore I will take up no more than is necessary. I am comforted to know that the Pennyfoot Hotel is in such capable hands."

Knowing him as well as she did, Cecily heard the irony in Baxter's voice. His sarcasm was apparently lost on Malcolm, however. He barely looked up from the open ledger in front of him as he muttered, "Thank you for stopping by, Mr. Baxter. I appreciate your offer, but I can assure you it is not necessary."

"I'm glad to hear it." Baxter leaned over the desk. "By the way, my good fellow, you might find it simpler to list all the housekeeping expenses in one column. Also, the cross balances should match the grand total of the end column. If I'm not mistaken, you have a difference of three shillings and sixpence."

Malcolm looked up, his eyes sparkling with anger. "I have not as yet reconciled the columns, Mr. Baxter. Thank you for pointing out the error. It will save me some time."

Baxter nodded. "Not at all. Glad to have been of some help."

He held the door open for Cecily, who brushed past him without looking at his face. Once outside, however, she faced him in the corridor.

"You are incorrigible, Baxter. You were positively preening when you pointed out his mistake. However did you manage to spot it?"

"It was simple enough to read the columns upside down."

"But your mental arithmetic is amazing. You added up those balances in your head faster than I could have written them down."

He smiled. "Thank you. It is always gratifying to have one's expertise appreciated."

She began walking down the narrow hallway, intensely aware of him just a step behind. "I always appreciated you, Baxter. I relied on you a great deal. I don't think I quite realized how much until you were no longer there."

He stopped her with a hand on her arm. She turned to face him, and he said quietly, "You always made me feel indispensable, Cecily. That is why it was so difficult to leave."

"But you have no regrets about leaving."

After a slight hesitation, he shrugged. "I rather miss our adventures. I have to admit, your determination to see justice done added quite a sense of excitement to my duties, even though you caused me a great deal of concern at times."

His words failed to warm her, though if she had been pressed for a reason, she couldn't have given one.

"I'm afraid I must leave now," she said. "I want to see the doctor before his waiting room is deserted."

Baxter's wistful expression vanished, to be replaced with an inscrutable look that reminded her of the old days.

Upon reaching the lobby, Ned Harris greeted her with a rather vulgar whistle of appreciation. "My, my," he exclaimed, "madam is looking very posh this afternoon. Might I have Samuel bring the trap around, or do you already have one waiting?" His gaze flicked over Baxter with avid curiosity.

"I have already ordered the trap, thank you, Ned."

Baxter, Cecily noticed, was looking at Ned as if he were something nasty swimming in his soup.

"This is Ned Harris, our new doorman," she said quickly.

"So I am informed." Baxter's tone was definitely caustic, but Ned appeared to take no offense.

"We met yesterday," Ned said with a cheerful grin. "It's a pleasure to see you again, sir."

Baxter merely nodded, then waited for Cecily to step out through the doors before following her. "What an uncouth fellow," he remarked when they were out of earshot. "He is far too familiar in his manner. That disgusting whistling was quite degrading."

Cecily felt obliged to defend her new doorman. "Actually I found it rather flattering."

She'd said the words more to tease him than anything, but Baxter's frown was formidable. "If I may say so, Cecily, I am surprised at your choice of employees since my departure. Malcolm Ridlington appears to be quite inadequate with figures, and your new doorman would do well to learn some decorum. While I am aware of how difficult it is to find suitable help these days, I hope you will not lower your standards."

"I agree that Ned has some rough edges." Cecily paused at the top of the steps and looked back at him. "But he is making an effort to improve, and his disposition is always pleasant and willing."

"Perhaps, but I should have been most wary about taking him on. What about his references? Were they respectable?"

"Quite," Cecily assured him. She had no intention of telling him that she had been unable to substantiate Ned's previous employment.

Baxter looked as if he didn't believe her.

"I'm sorry, Baxter," Cecily said quietly. "I must remind you that decisions such as these are no longer your concern. I can assure you, should either Malcolm Ridlington or Ned prove to be unworthy of the post I've entrusted to them, I shall not hesitate to dismiss them."

"I'm relieved to hear it," Baxter said, still looking put out.

Cecily sighed. She had the idea that Baxter's sudden bad humor was due more to the fact that she was on her way to see Dr. Prestwick than anything she might have said.

To make up for upsetting him, she gave him a warm smile. "If you are free this evening," she said impulsively, "perhaps you would care to join me for dinner? Michel is planning to serve turtle soup and roast venison, as well as that delicious princess pudding that you love so well."

He looked as if he might refuse, and her spirits drooped, only to rise again as his face relaxed in a smile. "I would enjoy that very much. Particularly if we could share a bottle of that excellent claret that Michel guards so zealously."

"I will have a bottle sent up for us," she promised him. He looked at her for a long moment, then reached for her hand. After drawing her fingers briefly to his lips, he murmured, "Until tonight, then."

She descended the steps to the waiting trap, aware of him watching her. She was impatient now to get the visit with Kevin Prestwick over as soon as possible. Much as she wanted to know what the doctor had found during his examination of Will Jones's body that was so suspicious, something else had taken precedence. Now she could hardly wait for tonight.

CHAPTER

❖ 10 ❖

"I am shocked that someone had the gall to actually steal something from a church," Phoebe declared as she and Algie stood gazing at the bogus relic. It had taken the vicar some time to convince her, but finally she had to admit that the dent in the side of the cup suggested it was made of far more fragile material than the heavy pewter of the original.

"Whatever are we going to do?" Algie moaned for at least the fifth time since he had announced the theft.

"It must have been stolen in the middle of the night and replaced with the fake," Phoebe murmured. "Though how someone got into the church after it was locked and bolted is a mystery to me. Especially since there appears to be no damage to the locks."

Algie stood wringing his hands, seemingly mesmerized by the replaced chalice.

"I simply can't imagine anyone risking such a thing in broad daylight," Phoebe declared. "One or the other of us has been inside this church every single day since the chalice was placed here."

"Whatever are we going to do?" Algie moaned once again.

Phoebe turned on him. "For heaven's sake, Algie, pull yourself together. We have to report the theft to P.C. Northcott, of course."

She looked back at the cup. Now that she knew it was a fake, it actually looked quite tawdry. "Of course," she added, "it could have been stolen while everyone was at the Pennyfoot for the St. Bartholomew's Feast. The church would have been empty then, and it wasn't locked until we returned."

"We can't report this to the constable," Algie said, tearing his gaze away from the glass case. "We can't let the b-bishop know the cup is missing."

Phoebe sighed. "I hardly think the bishop is going to be fooled by this fake for long."

"We m-must find the right one, then," Algie said, looking about him as if he thought the chalice was hidden somewhere in the church.

"How do you propose we do that?" Phoebe demanded. "We have not the slightest idea where to start."

"We have . . . ah . . . three days before the b-bishop comes to collect the chalice," Algie said, giving her an imploring look. "Surely we can find it before then?"

"I seriously doubt it. Whoever took it must be far away by now."

"Then we have to find out who took it and try to get it back."

"We might just as well try to fly to the moon. We must tell the constable and let him try to find the thief. He knows how to go about it."

"But he'll tell the b-bishop!"

Algie's voice had risen to a squeak, and Phoebe viewed him with alarm. "Please calm down, Algie. You know what happens when you get excited. I really don't think you want to conduct the clipping and the service on Friday with those nasty red blotches all over your face."

"I forgot about the service!" Algie looked as if he were about to expire. "Everyone will be staring at the chalice. Someone is bound to notice the dent in it. Everyone will know it's a fake." He buried his head in his hands. "I am ruined. The b-bishop will banish me from the ministry. My life in the ministry is over."

"Nonsense," Phoebe said briskly, "we'll turn the case around so that the dent cannot be seen from the pews. That way, no one will notice."

Algie lifted his head, a glimmer of hope in his eyes. "Will that give us enough time to find out who took it?"

Phoebe was of the opinion that a year would not be long enough, but she refrained from saying so. "It might be a little difficult to find the thief by ourselves. Suppose I ask the constable not to say anything to the bishop, at least until he's ready to leave on Saturday? Perhaps P.C. Northcott will be able to find the culprit by then."

"No, no, no!" Algie shook his head so hard his glasses slipped from his nose. Catching them as they fell, he sounded close to tears when he mumbled, "The constable will feel it is his duty to inform him. You know how he is."

"Oh, very well." There was no point in arguing with him in any case, she thought, since it was a foregone conclusion that the bishop would have to know about the theft sooner or later. Struck by an idea, she uttered a soft exclamation.

Apparently seized by even this tiny glimmer of salvation, Algie clutched her arm. "What? What are you thinking? Tell me!"

"I don't know how much good it would do," Phoebe admitted, hating to douse the hope shimmering on her son's face, "but I could have a word with Cecily. You know how clever she is with problems such as this. Perhaps she can track down our thief before Saturday."

"Yes, yes, ask her," Algie urged, his face now alight with relief. "If anyone can find the thief, Mrs. Sinclair can do it. Just be sure you insist that she not tell the b-bishop."

"Don't worry," Phoebe said, reaching for her parasol. "Cecily won't breathe a word. I will go and see her this afternoon and explain what has happened. Perhaps she will be able to help us."

"I certainly hope so," Algie muttered, sending an accusing gaze at the offending fake, "because if not, Mother, you and I could very well be out on the s-street."

"My dear, you look absolutely ravishing," Kevin Prestwick proclaimed when Cecily was ushered into his office by his smiling receptionist. "What have you done to yourself? You look years younger than when I last saw you."

Cecily acknowledged the compliments with a slight bow of her head. She knew better than to take the attractive doctor's lavish comments too seriously. He paid similar attention to just about every woman who came into contact with him.

"It is a pleasure to see you, as always, Kevin," she said, taking the chair he pulled back for her. "We missed you at the feast on Monday."

"Unfortunately I had an emergency in Wellercombe." The doctor seated himself at his desk again and folded his hands in front of him. "You are looking positively radiant, my dear. I trust you are well?"

"Very well, thank you, Doctor." Cecily met his wary gaze with a smile. "And you?"

"Quite well, all things considered." He paused, watching her thoughtfully. "I take it, then, that you are not here to discuss a problem with your health?"

Knowing that to pretend otherwise would be a waste of time, Cecily said cheerfully, "I'm sure you can guess why I'm here."

"I imagine it has something to do with the recent tragic death of Will Jones."

"Precisely. P.C. Northcott informed me that you examined his body."

Kevin Prestwick looked amused. "You manage to charm even our stalwart police officers into divulging their secrets, I see."

Cecily gave him a look of mock disdain. "P.C. Northcott would tell his secrets to the entire village if he thought it would make him appear important."

"You're probably right." Prestwick leaned back in his chair and steepled his hands. "I, on the other hand, need a little more persuading. As you well know, I cannot discuss the details of a police case with anyone."

"I do know that, Kevin." Cecily leaned forward and gave him her most winning smile. "If I should ask a few questions, however, and you happened to nod or shake your head occasionally, no one could take exception with that, now could they?"

The doctor's grin widened. "You really are irresistible, my dear. When are you going to come to your senses and allow me to court you? I promise you won't be disappointed."

Cecily dropped her gaze, pretending to fuss with her

glove. "I can assure you, Kevin, you would very soon tire of me. I have some quite appalling habits that would no doubt try a saint."

"Why don't you let me be the judge of that?"

She looked up and met his gaze. "Did I happen to mention that Baxter is in Badgers End for the celebrations?"

His smile faded just a little. "So I have heard. You are still attached to your invincible manager, is that it? I was hoping that you would recover from that infatuation after a while."

He had spoken lightly enough, yet Cecily detected an underlying regret in his words. She smiled at him and said quietly, "I would hardly call my regard for Baxter an infatuation."

"I do hope you are not seriously enamored of the man. He would not know how to appreciate a woman such as you."

She shook her head at him. "If you were not such a good friend, Kevin, I would tell you to mind your own business."

"It is because I am such a good friend that I am concerned for your welfare." He looked suddenly serious. "I would not wish to see you hurt, Cecily."

"I have no intention of being hurt," she assured him. "I am in complete control of the situation. Now, about the matter of Will Jones."

Prestwick looked at her for a long moment, then sighed. "I can't promise to tell you what you want to know."

"I know that his death is being considered a murder. P.C. Northcott told me that much."

The doctor raised his eyebrows. "The constable was certainly informative. What else did he tell you?"

"He mentioned the fact that Bernard Willoughby had heard Will fall, and that he'd heard footsteps after the splash. He also told me that you found something suspicious during your examination."

"But he didn't say what it was."

Cecily picked a piece of white fluff from her glove. "No, he didn't. I was wondering if it was something incriminating, however, since he was so secretive about that part."

There was a long pause, broken by a ripple of laughter from the waiting room outside. Cecily looked up to see the doctor regarding her gravely.

"I do hope that you are not intending to continue your escapades alone," he said with a frown. "I shouldn't have to remind you how dangerous that could be."

"I have no intention of putting myself in danger." She glanced at the large clock hanging on the wall. "I have taken up too much of your time as it is, Kevin. I merely want to know if Will's death was murder, as P.C. Northcott implied."

"Since he's told you that much, I might as well tell you the rest. What little there is to tell." Prestwick reached for a sheet of paper and drew it toward him. "Will's lungs contained no water, suggesting he died before he landed in the ocean. A severe injury to his head was the probable cause of death."

"I see." Cecily considered what she had heard, then added, "Could he not have hit his head on the rocks and died before slipping into the water?"

"Not at that time of night. It was high tide. If Will had been alive when he fell from the cliff, he would have hit the water before reaching the rocks. I would say that whoever attacked him hit him with a heavy object, hard enough to kill him, then pushed him over the cliff."

Cecily shook her head. "Whoever would do a thing like that to poor Will? He was one of the kindest, gentlest men I have ever met. I can't believe someone would have a reason to murder him."

"Some people don't need a reason." Prestwick got up from his chair and moved around the desk to place his hand on Cecily's shoulder. "If someone did hit that poor old gentleman on the head, the murderer might well have been either intoxicated or disturbed in the mind. Or both."

Cecily stood, allowing the doctor to pull back her chair. "I have to agree with you, Kevin. I only hope that the gypsies have not returned to plague us again. Though I have to admit that as yet they have not been responsible for anything as abominable as taking an innocent man's life."

Dr. Prestwick took hold of her arm to escort her to the door. "It never fails to amaze me, my dear, how intensely you abhor the taking of a life, considering you were a military wife for many years."

Cecily lifted her chin. "There is a very great difference in taking a life in war, when the safety of your own life and perhaps your country is at stake. Even so, I found it hard to accept the necessity."

"I imagine you did." Prestwick opened the door for her. "It was good to see you again, Cecily. I hope I shall see you at the church on Friday?"

She looked up at him with a quick smile. "You are coming to the clipping? How nice. Phoebe will be happy to see you there."

"Thank you, my dear. I hope that applies to you also. I just hope I don't run into your ex-manager. He does not approve of me, I fear."

"Baxter is no longer in my employ," Cecily said crisply. "Whatever he does or does not approve of is of no interest to me."

Kevin gave her a smile that must have made every heart in the waiting room beat more swiftly. "I would feel a great deal better if you could say that with a little more conviction. As you have pointed out to me, however, it is none of my business."

Aware that the ears of everyone in the waiting room were

trained on their every word, Cecily merely nodded. "Thank you, Doctor, for your help. It is most appreciated."

She held out her hand, and the doctor took it, lifting it to his lips briefly before letting her go. "Until Friday, then, my dear."

Crossing the waiting room, Cecily exchanged smiles with the women seated there, every one of them, she was sure, anxiously awaiting their turn to be charmed by the magnetic doctor.

Why was it, she wondered as Samuel helped her up into the trap, that one man could pay her so much unwanted attention, while another didn't give her nearly enough? Though she had to admit, this past day or two Baxter had been unusually attentive. If only she knew what that meant.

Settling back in the trap, she allowed herself the luxury of looking forward to sharing her dinner table that evening with her ex-manager.

Her pleasant thoughts lasted all the way back to the hotel. So intent was she on deciding what to wear that evening that she barely heard Samuel when he asked if he could have a word with her.

Gathering her senses, she was immediately concerned by the worried expression on her stable manager's face. "What is it, Samuel?"

"Begging your pardon, mum, but I thought you ought to know. I should have told you before but I didn't want to interrupt your visit with the doctor."

"It's all right, Samuel. Just tell me now what the problem seems to be."

"It's the trap, mum."

Cecily sent a startled glance at the trap. "There's something wrong with it?"

"Not this one, mum, the other one." Samuel stood twisting his cap miserably in his hands. "I think someone took it out on Monday night. I don't know who it was, but they weren't too careful with it. The right rear wheel has a wedge taken right out of it."

Now he had Cecily's entire attention. "Are you certain it was Monday night?"

"Yes, mum." Samuel nodded earnestly. "I noticed some dirt on the back seat when I got back from the feast, and I'd cleaned both the traps before going to the dining room. Then, when I cleaned the trap again this morning, I found this big gash in the wheel. Looks like someone took a corner a little too sharp, that's what I think."

"Well, everyone was in the dining room that night for the feast . . ." No, not everyone, she thought. Malcolm Ridlington was absent, for one.

"Did you mention this to Mr. Ridlington?" she asked Samuel, who fidgeted from one foot to the other as if he were wishing he were somewhere else.

"Yes, mum, I did. I thought as how he might be the one what took it. But he said he was in the office all night working on the books. Weren't none too happy about it neither."

"Perhaps one of the village boys took it for a lark," Cecily said. "Perhaps we shall have to lock up the stables at night."

"I think it must have been someone from the hotel, mum," Samuel said unhappily. "When I was cleaning it out I found one of them chocolate mint sweets that Doris put in all the rooms for the guests."

Cecily gave him a sharp look. "Thank you, Samuel. I'll have a word with Mr. Ridlington myself about the matter. In the meantime, see about getting the wheel repaired."

"Yes, mum. Though I'm thinking we might have to get it replaced."

"Very well, Samuel. Whatever has to be done."

Samuel pulled his cap back on and reached for the

chestnut's bridle. "It weren't me, mum, honest. I'm a careful driver, I am. I've never hit anything in me life. Honest to God, I haven't."

"It's all right, Samuel," Cecily assured him. "I'm quite sure we'll get to the bottom of this matter. Please don't worry."

"Yes, mum. Thank you, mum." Looking a little less desperate, Samuel slowly led the horse and trap back to the stable.

Cecily watched him go, the frown still on her face. The last person to mention the dinner mints was the colonel. What was it Kevin Prestwick had said? *The murderer might well have been either intoxicated or disturbed in the mind. Or both.*

CHAPTER

❖ 11 ❖

Cecily was enjoying a few quiet moments with a pot of tea in her suite when Doris tapped on her door to announce the arrival of Phoebe.

Anxiously waiting for her friend, Cecily wondered if she had further news of Will Jones, or if, indeed, Phoebe was aware that Will was murdered.

Deciding not to say anything unless the subject came up, Cecily welcomed her guest. "Would you care for some tea?" she asked as Phoebe fussily settled herself in her favorite Queen Anne chair.

"I would love some, Cecily, thank you. It is rather warm outside, and I always find tea so refreshing after a long walk." She hunted in her sleeve for her handkerchief and delicately fanned her pink face. "Thank heaven for these

giant brims on hats these days. It certainly does help to keep
the sun off one's face."

"It does, indeed." Cecily turned to Doris, who was
politely hovering in the doorway waiting to be dismissed.
"Please bring up a fresh pot of tea for two and some
sandwiches and cakes for Mrs. Carter-Holmes."

"Yes, mum." Doris bobbed a curtsey and disappeared.

"Oh, how nice, Cecily," Phoebe murmured. "We haven't
had afternoon tea together in quite a while."

"No, we haven't." Cecily took a seat on her chaise lounge
and looked expectantly at Phoebe. "Now, what brings you
here in the middle of the week? I trust the plans for the
clipping are going well?"

"Oh, my dear." Phoebe touched a corner of her handkerchief to her brow. "Don't even mention the clipping. Those
dreadful girls are bound to make utter chaos of the entire
ceremony, as usual. I can't imagine why Algie insists on
continuing with it, after he witnessed the debacle they made
of it this morning. And now there's this business with the
chalice . . ."

"The chalice?"

Phoebe carefully folded her handkerchief again. "I'm
afraid something rather dreadful has happened to it."

"Oh, Lord, no," Cecily exclaimed. "Whatever happened?"

Phoebe's bosom heaved as she drew in a long breath and
then let it out on a long sigh. "Cecily, I know this will shock
you as much as it did Algie and me. I'm afraid . . ."

She paused, apparently for dramatic effect. Cecily curbed
her impatience.

"I'm afraid, Cecily," Phoebe said when it became apparent that Cecily was not going to beg for the details, "that the
chalice has been . . . stolen!" This last word was accompanied by a theatrical flourish that flipped the handkerchief
open again.

Cecily stared at her in disbelief. Well used to Phoebe's melodramatic statements, she had not expected a genuine disaster. "Great heavens, Phoebe, however did that happen? Wasn't the chalice under lock and key?"

Phoebe blinked. "Well, yes, now that you mention it, it certainly was. Nevertheless, someone managed to unlock the case and replace the real chalice with a shoddy fake. Algie noticed it when he caught the case as it was falling to the floor."

"It fell?" Cecily said, trying to make sense of all this.

"Yes. One of those dreadful creatures tried to take it off the pedestal for a closer look. The case slipped, and Algie, in a most spectacular display of agility, I might say, managed to catch it before it hit the floor. He noticed it wasn't as heavy as when he'd assisted the bishop in placing it on the pedestal."

Cecily sat back, shaking her head. "I think it's entirely possible that Algie is mistaken. You know how excited he gets when faced with a calamity."

"I do, indeed," Phoebe said, tucking her handkerchief back into her sleeve. "However—" She broke off as a sharp tap sounded on the door.

"Come in!" Cecily called out.

The door opened slowly as Doris struggled in with the loaded tray. Phoebe sat quietly, her gaze intent on the three-tiered dish of elegant sandwiches and cakes, as Doris carefully laid the tray down on the polished round table and set out the fragile bone china cups and saucers.

"Shall I pour, mum?" the maid asked as she removed the large silver teapot from the tray and set it down on the stand.

"Thank you, Doris, but I'll manage." Cecily waited for her to set out the silver bowl of sugar lumps, the tiny jug of milk, and the larger jug of hot water to refill the teapot.

After placing a small plate in front of both women, Doris

then offered the cake dish to Phoebe, who took an inordinate amount of time in making her selection. Finally she reached for a dainty crustless sandwich filled with soft roe and tomato and another with cheese and cucumber.

Cecily chose an egg and cress sandwich, seasoned with curry powder, then waited until the girl had left the room before reaching for the milk jug. "Now, Phoebe," she said as she poured a minute amount into each cup, "you were saying?"

"I was saying," Phoebe said, "that I thought Algie was imagining things, too, at first. But then he showed me a rather large dent in the side of the chalice, which must have happened when it fell. It certainly wasn't there before."

Cecily looked up, the jug poised in her hand. "A dent?"

"Yes." Phoebe took a small bite out of her sandwich and munched with obvious enjoyment before swallowing the morsel. "I really must commend Altheda Chubb on her bread. Quite delectable."

"You mentioned a dent," Cecily reminded her. She was beginning to develop a nasty suspicion that there might be some substance to Phoebe's assertion of a theft after all.

"Oh, yes. The dent. Well, you see, it couldn't possibly be the real chalice. That is made of pewter an inch thick. As Algie so aptly put it, it would take a sledgehammer to put a dent in it. Algie surmises that this one is made of tin."

"Tin?" Cecily made an effort to grasp the enormity of what Phoebe was telling her. "Phoebe, if the chalice was really stolen, that would be a disaster. It must be priceless— quite irreplaceable, I would say."

"Oh, quite." Phoebe finished the sandwich and reached for another. "That is why I am here, Cecily dear. We would like you to help us find it."

Cecily put the jug down so quickly some milk slopped over the side. "I really think the police should be looking for it, and as soon as possible. We are wasting valuable time sitting here chatting about it. The thief could be far away with it by now."

Phoebe finished her mouthful of sandwich. "Algie insists that we not report this to the constable. He is afraid the bishop will find out before we recover the cup."

Cecily felt like shaking her friend. "Phoebe, the bishop must be informed of the theft at once."

"Oh, no," Phoebe said vehemently. "Algie has absolutely forbidden me to mention it to the bishop." She looked anxious again as she stared at Cecily. "I promised him you wouldn't say anything to anyone. Please, Cecily, you really mustn't."

"I don't think you understand the seriousness of this," Cecily began, but Phoebe interrupted her.

"Oh, I do, I do. Why, Algie is quite distraught, I can promise you." She helped herself to an almond-cherry tart. "Algie and I think the chalice was stolen on Monday night while everyone was at the feast. That's the only time, except for after dark, of course, that the church was left unlocked and unattended."

Cecily lifted her hands in a helpless gesture. "The cup is more than likely out of the country by now. It's extremely unlikely that it can be recovered before Saturday. You will have to tell the bishop then."

Phoebe reached for a serviette and dabbed at her mouth. "Yes, I suppose we shall. Then again, I really don't think we can be blamed for a theft from the church. The bishop quite clearly secured the glass case himself. Surely he should be held responsible if his efforts were inadequate to prevent a theft? After all, we should not be expected to stand watch all day and night."

"That's not the point," Cecily said in exasperation. "By keeping quiet about the theft, you are compounding the problem. If we report it to the proper authorities, they might be able to do something about it."

"We can't do that. Algie would have a fit. He's over-wrought as it is, with all this happening two days before the ceremony. I really can't have him upset any more." She leaned forward and patted Cecily's knee. "Personally, I think he's worrying about nothing. While I agree that the theft of such a valuable article is a tragedy, as I've said already, we can't possible be blamed for it."

She sat up and reached for a slice of walnut cream cake. "To be perfectly honest, I believe you can find it. You are always so clever at these things."

"I am flattered by your confidence in me," Cecily said carefully. "But I have to tell you, Phoebe, I really doubt that I can find your thief for you in three days."

Phoebe sighed. "Well, if you can't, you can't. Algie and I will just have to accept the consequences, I suppose." She lifted her cup and took a few sips of tea. "You will do your best, though, won't you? I'm afraid that Algie will be beside himself if the chalice isn't found by Saturday."

"I'll do what I can," Cecily said, wondering where on earth she was going to start. She had enough trouble on her hands trying to discover what happened to Will Jones. Again she wondered if Phoebe knew that he was murdered. It didn't seem the right time to tell her, in any case.

"Thank you, Cecily. I knew I could count on you." Phoebe finished her tea and set her cup down in the saucer. "You haven't eaten hardly anything. Are you not well?"

"I'm quite well, thank you. I would rather not spoil my appetite for my evening meal, that's all."

"Well, I certainly hope you eat more than that tonight." Phoebe rose and smoothed down her skirt. "I must be off, Cecily. Algie was quite upset when I left. I don't want to leave him alone too long. Thank you for agreeing to help us. I'm sure it will be a relief to Algie."

"Please, don't expect too much," Cecily warned as she accompanied her to the door. "I can't promise that I'll be of any help at all. I still think you should be talking to P.C. Northcott."

"Yes, well, so do I, actually. But Algie was adamant, I'm afraid." She reached the door and waited for Cecily to open it. "Don't come down with me—I'll find my own way out. I've taken up enough of your time as it is." She gave Cecily a sly look. "I heard that Mr. Baxter has returned. Would you be having dinner with him tonight, by any chance?"

Cecily felt a flutter in her stomach, which she immediately put down to hunger. "As a matter of fact, I am. We have a lot to discuss, since Malcolm is having so much trouble with the bookkeeping."

"Yes, well, enjoy yourself, my dear." Phoebe's smile was smug as she stepped out into the hallway.

Cecily closed the door, wishing she hadn't admitted to her appointment with Baxter. It would be just like Phoebe to misconstrue the meeting and blow it all out of proportion.

Which was something she herself had to guard against, she thought as she tugged on the velvet bell rope to summon a maid. She had merely invited an acquaintance to dinner, and naturally he had accepted. It would have been churlish not to accept, under the circumstances.

Now that she came to think about it, the invitation had been rather forward of her. Ordinarily ladies did not invite gentlemen to dine with them. When Baxter had worked for her, she had often asked him to join her for a meal, usually to discuss some problem in the hotel that had arisen. She had thought nothing of it at the time.

Baxter no longer worked at the hotel, however, and she had twice invited him to join her. The fact that he had accepted, apparently without any qualms and most certainly without his usual chiding about her modern attitude, would certainly suggest that his own perspective had gone through a drastic change.

The thought did little to calm her nerves, and by the time she was dressing for dinner that evening in a gown of pale blue imported batiste, her hands trembled so badly that she had to summon help to fasten the garment in the back.

Doris arrived to assist her, exclaiming with admiration over the *point de Paris* lace collar and princess panel down the front of her gown.

"It is the most beautiful frock I've ever set me eyes on, mum," she declared, fastening the tiny buttons in the back. "I'd like to wear one just like this when I go on the stage."

"I'm sure you will," Cecily said, smiling at the maid's image in the mirror. "In fact, one far better than this, I shouldn't wonder."

"You really think so?" Doris's eyes were full of hope, and Cecily felt a pang of sympathy. How well she knew what it was to hold onto a dream, no matter how impossible it seemed.

"I really think so," she said firmly. "Thank you for your help, Doris. I can manage the rest."

"Yes, mum." Doris sped happily out of the door and closed it gently behind her.

Cecily stared at her hair in the mirror. Perhaps she should have enlisted Doris's help with it, after all, she thought, after she'd fussed with it for another ten minutes.

Finally she was ready. It really was ridiculous to feel this jittery about meeting one's ex-employee, she told herself sternly. The scolding didn't seem to help, however. Especially when she walked downstairs and found Baxter waiting for her at the bottom.

He watched her descend the last few steps, while she tried

to appear nonchalant and composed. As she reached the last one, he held out his hand to assist her.

"May I say that I have never seen you look so lovely, Cecily, " he said, and lifted her gloved hand to his lips.

As always, the gesture brought back the annoying fluttering in her heart. "Thank you, Baxter," she murmured. "You look quite dashing yourself." It was an understatement. Baxter in a black dinner suit and crisp white shirt looked quite majestic.

His smile seemed to have a peculiar effect on her breathing. She took his proffered arm and attempted to relax as he escorted her down the hallway to the dining room, where the orchestra was playing a soft, lilting melody.

Seated with him at her corner table, she did her best to appear calm and composed. It wouldn't do to let him know how unsettling she found his presence.

She watched him pour his favorite claret into the crystal wine glass, then lift his glass to propose a toast. "To a woman," he said softly, "I admire above all others."

Her heart seemed to be racing at twice its normal speed. What exactly did he mean by those words? Baxter could be so infuriatingly obtuse at times. Could he actually be serious and intending to court her after all?

Her hand shook as she lifted her own glass, but she managed to take a sip before setting it down again. Now that she was actually considering the prospect, she wasn't at all sure how she felt.

For so long she had nursed her affection for Baxter, tormented by secret longings that seemed unlikely to ever bear fruit. The idea that he could finally be reciprocating those feelings filled her with misgivings. She had dreamed of his proposal of marriage but never really believed it could happen. Now she wasn't at all sure what she would do if he actually asked her to marry him.

"You are looking unduly pensive."

She started, aware that she had been staring into space for too long. "I'm sorry, Baxter, I'm afraid my thoughts wandered elsewhere. I have a lot on my mind this evening."

"I can see I shall have to find more stimulating conversation if I am to hold your interest."

Immediately contrite, Cecily gave him a warm smile. "Forgive me, Baxter, I promise you shall have my undivided attention from now on."

His serious air gave her cause for concern. "I hope so, Cecily, for this night could be of great significance."

If only she could read the expression on his face, she thought in despair. Perhaps then she would know better how to deal with whatever was on his mind.

Whatever it was, she had the uncomfortable feeling that after tonight nothing between her and Baxter was ever going to be the same again.

CHAPTER

❊ 12 ❊

Deciding it was safer to change the subject for the time being, Cecily sipped her wine, then said brightly, "You haven't asked me what I learned from Dr. Prestwick."

Baxter studied his glass for a moment. "I assumed that sooner or later you would tell me what you wanted me to hear."

Piqued by his apparent disinterest, Cecily frowned. "It would seem that your thirst for adventure has been quenched by your new vocation. There was a time when you would have been panting to know."

He looked up then, and she was disconcerted by the gleam in his eye. "I did not wish to seem inquisitive about something that did not concern me; that is all."

"Oh." Feeling slightly at a loss, Cecily reached for a plate of hors d'oeuvres and offered it to him. He took a square of toast spread with soft roe and cucumber. After a moment of indecision, she chose the crab paste and cress.

"I am interested, Cecily, in anything that concerns you. As always, I would hope that you would not go chasing after a murderous thug, but from long experience I know full well the futility of cautioning you on the subject."

"Well, in this case, I think you may rest assured that the thug in question is quite harmless." She stared at the morsel on her plate without touching it. "At least, I've always thought so."

Baxter heaved a heavy sigh. "Very well, you now have whetted my curiosity to the point where I'm compelled to ask. What did you learn from that idiot, Prestwick?"

Deciding to allow him his opinion of the doctor, Cecily said mildly, "It seems that P.C. Northcott is right for once. Will Jones was dead when he landed in the water Monday night. Apparently Will suffered a severe blow to the head that most likely killed him. Dr. Prestwick says he couldn't have hit his head on the rocks below since the tide was in at the time. In any case, there was no water in his lungs."

"He couldn't have hit his head on the way down?"

Cecily shook her head. "He fell into the Devil's Cauldron. As you know, the cliff juts out over the ocean there. He would have fallen directly into the water."

Baxter made a small sound of disgust. "I must confess, until now I thought perhaps Will had died of a heart attack or something similar that would explain his falling over the cliff. I simply can't imagine why someone would want to kill that poor old man."

"That's an important point, I think," Cecily said unhappily. "The doctor thinks whoever did it could have been drunk or mentally disturbed. Perhaps both."

Baxter gave her an intent look. "I see. You are thinking it could be someone we both know?"

Cecily nodded. "Colonel Fortescue."

Baxter raised his eyebrows, then gave a decisive shake of his head. "Forgive me, Cecily, I find that extremely difficult to believe. While I must admit, there have been times when the colonel has given me cause to doubt his stability, there has always been some kind of reasoning behind his actions."

"I know." She toyed absently with the edge of her plate. "But with the absence of a motive, what else am I to think?"

"That Colonel Fortescue is not the only person in the world to have a disturbed mind."

"Perhaps not." She looked up at him, reluctant to put into words what her mind had conceived. "Samuel tells me someone borrowed a trap on the night of St. Bartholomew's Feast. He found a chocolate mint sweet on the seat, the kind that I had provided for the guests in their rooms. The colonel mentioned that he enjoyed those sweets."

"So, I presume, do many of the guests."

"True. But the colonel was not at the feast that night. He said he forgot about it, yet it isn't like him to forget such a festive occasion."

Baxter sighed. "Cecily, the colonel would forget his own name if people didn't keep mentioning it."

"Also," Cecily went on doggedly, "the colonel told me himself that he was fifteen minutes late arriving at the pub that night. I believe he borrowed the trap because he realized he was going to be late. You know how erratic he is. He might have run down Will Jones on the path, realized what he'd done, and dropped him over the side so that everyone would think Will had fallen over."

"And then he told you he was late arriving at the pub, thereby putting suspicion on himself."

Cecily shrugged. "I admit it sounds ludicrous, but he could have forgotten it ever happened."

She was surprised and quite flustered when Baxter reached out and covered her hand with his. "For once you are not using your excellent powers of reasoning. Consider the facts. Everyone in this hotel had access to the sweets. And if I remember correctly, several people were missing the night of the feast, including that manly Miss Parsons as well as your own manager, Malcolm Ridlington."

"And Sid Barker," Cecily said, unsettled by Baxter's apparent lack of concern as to what people would say about the intimate gesture. At that very moment one of her waiters was heading toward their table.

Fortunately Baxter noticed, as he removed his hand and reached for his wine glass.

While the waiter laid out the dishes in front of them, Cecily nibbled on her crab canapé, giving thought to Baxter's words. After the waiter had left, she gave Baxter a rueful smile. "I'm afraid you may well be right, Baxter. I seem to have mislaid my usual perception in this case. I suppose I have been somewhat distracted lately and I haven't been giving the situation my full concentration."

"Perhaps you are working too hard." He studied her for a moment. "Now that you mention it, you do seem somewhat perturbed tonight. I trust you are allowing your new manager to take up his share of the duties?"

"I am not overworked, Baxter. I simply have a lot on my mind, that's all. I don't know why I should pick on the colonel. After all, the truth of the matter is, he most likely dawdled more than usual that night, even though he did insist he kept up his normal pace."

"More than likely. Fortescue is not exactly reliable at the best of times." Baxter gave his meal an appreciative inspection. "Michel has lost none of his expertise, I'm happy to say."

"It does seem odd, though," Cecily murmured, reluctant to let go of the subject, "that it should be the very night of a murder that the colonel was late. I remember my son telling me when he owned the George and Dragon that people could tell the time by the colonel's punctuality."

"I don't know how he can possibly be punctual when he doesn't wear a watch." Baxter gave her a look of mock severity. "Don't you think you should start your meal before it gets cold?"

Cecily obediently picked up her knife and fork. The wine had relaxed her a little, and she was looking forward to enjoying her meal. The puzzle of Colonel Fortescue's tardiness could wait.

"There's something else I haven't told you," she said as she tackled the delicious-looking salmon on her plate. "I promised Phoebe I wouldn't tell anyone, but I know you can be trusted not to say anything."

Baxter gave her a sardonic look. "What has Mrs. Carter-Holmes been up to now? Let me hazard a guess. She set fire to the village hall while teaching her abominable dance troupe to leap through a ring of flames, perhaps?"

Cecily grinned. "Not quite. This time she wasn't responsible for the catastrophe."

"Well, that's a refreshing change."

Cecily's smile faded. "It is rather serious, though." She looked around to make sure no one was listening. The guests at the nearest table appeared to be chattering quite earnestly amongst themselves. Anyone else was too far away from her table in the corner to overhear anything she might say.

Leaning forward, she said in a conspiratorial whisper, "The Helmsboro chalice has been stolen."

Baxter looked startled. "Stolen?"

"Shssh!" Cecily held a finger across her lips. "It's supposed to be a secret."

"Is the bishop aware of that?"

"Of course not. That's the point." Again Cecily looked around before whispering, "Algie doesn't want the bishop to know. He's hoping the chalice can be found before Saturday."

"If it's left up to Northcott it will be doomsday before it's found. The bishop will have to know eventually."

Cecily finished another mouthful of salmon. "Yes, well, I'm afraid the constable doesn't know about it, either. Algie wants me to find it."

Carefully Baxter laid down his knife and fork. Reaching for his serviette, he blotted his mouth. "Unbelievable."

Cecily felt a little hurt. "I have been known to solve a puzzle now and again."

"Undoubtedly. Common theft is not your forte, however, is it? How do you propose to go about looking for the thief? And how is the vicar going to explain the absence of the chalice at the service on Friday?"

"Apparently the thief replaced the real chalice with a fake one."

Cecily watched warily as Baxter paused, his fork halfway to his mouth. "A fake chalice. Ingenious. It must be a very poor substitute for our obtuse vicar to detect it."

"He said it wasn't as heavy as the other one."

"Not as heavy."

"No."

"He lifted it up to determine its weight?"

"Not exactly. One of the dance troupe dropped it and—"

"Aha! I suspected that bevy of buffoons had something to do with it."

"Baxter, you are not taking this seriously."

He placed the fork in his mouth and chewed with obvious

enjoyment before swallowing. "You are asking me to take the word of the Reverend Algernon Carter-Holmes seriously?"

"Phoebe says there's a dent in it."

"A dent. In the chalice?"

"Yes." His patronizing manner began to irritate her. She leaned forward again and said deliberately, "Do you have any idea, Baxter, what it would take to put a dent in a chalice made of inch-thick pewter? The dent wasn't there when the bishop left the chalice. It is there now."

"Perhaps the vicar didn't see the dent until after the girl dropped it." He shook his head slightly, as if wondering why he was participating in this particular discussion.

"Both Phoebe and Algie are convinced it wasn't there. I'm inclined to believe them."

"Is the case a fake, too?"

"I don't know." She wondered why that hadn't occurred to her. "I suppose it could be. But then the thief would have had to unlock the chain around the pedestal."

"And if not, he would have had to unlock the case itself."

Cecily sighed. "I know it sounds impossible, but Phoebe seems so certain. I promised her I would do what I could."

Baxter laid down his knife and fork with a sigh of satisfaction. "Excellent, as always."

"I'm glad you enjoyed it so much."

He must have caught the note of reproof in her voice as he gave her a sharp look. "Cecily, if Mrs. Carter-Holmes is correct in her assumption that the chalice has been"—he dropped his voice—"stolen, I fail to see what you can do about it before Saturday."

"I know." Cecily lifted her hands in a gesture of defeat. "But what could I say? She is a friend in need of my help."

Baxter's expression softened. "And, as always, you feel compelled to offer that help. No matter the cost. It's no wonder you are looking tired, Cecily. What with worrying about Colonel Fortescue and Will Jones and the vicar and his mother as well, your mind must be in a complete turmoil."

She was looking tired? She'd barely heard the rest of the sentence. After all that primping in front of the mirror, all she'd managed was to look tired?

"I may be wrong about the colonel," she began defensively and then paused, remembering something that gentleman had said to her. "Colonel Fortescue insisted that he left at the same time as usual," she continued as Baxter watched her curiously. "He timed it by the sound of the church bells. He also insisted that he kept his usual pace. In fact, he seemed quite confused as to why he'd arrived late."

"If I might be permitted to say so, confused is the colonel's usual state of mind."

Cecily felt a little catch of excitement. "Maybe. But when it comes to arriving at the George and Dragon, he is always on time. He's been walking down to the pub at night for years. Habits are very hard to break."

"Particularly drunken habits."

"Baxter, please."

He sighed. "Forgive me. What is your point?"

Cecily sat up straight in her chair. "I had assumed, as anyone would, that the bells were rung at the usual time of half past seven. But supposing they weren't rung then? Supposing the bells were rung fifteen minutes later? That would explain why the colonel arrived at the pub later than usual."

"Perhaps," Baxter said slowly. "But then, why would Will ring the bells later than usual? In fact, why would he ring them at all, since the service had been cancelled because of the feast that night?"

"I don't think he did." Cecily gave him a smug smile.

"Let us suppose that Will wasn't killed up on the cliffs after all. Let us suppose that he surprised the thief in the act of stealing the chalice at the church. The thief killed Will to silence him, then, thinking that the bells had to be rung, rang them himself before taking Will's body up to the cliffs."

Baxter gave her a long look. "I retract my statement about your lack of perception. I can see you are as sharp as ever."

"Thank you, Bax. That means a lot to me."

"There's just one small point."

Her smile subsided a little. "What's that?"

"Why would the thief assume that the bells had to be rung?"

"If he doesn't live in the village, he wouldn't know that the bells are rung to remind the villagers of the evening service. He might have heard them the evening before and assumed they were rung every evening at that time."

"Which they usually are."

"Except on the rare occasion when there's no evening service."

"Which means," Baxter said quietly, "that the thief is most likely a visitor."

"Yes," Cecily said, feeling depressed all of a sudden. "And more than likely he is staying in this hotel."

"Cecily, you must tell the constable. Not that I have an enormous amount of respect for the local constabulary, but at least you won't be responsible for allowing a thief, and possibly a murderer, to get away."

"Almost certainly a murderer. I feel quite certain now that if we find the chalice we shall also find whoever killed Will Jones."

"All the more reason for you to inform the police," Baxter said, looking worried. "Up until now I had not taken this matter seriously, but now it seems as if there might be some truth to your suspicions. I implore you to let the constabulary handle it."

Cecily shook her head. "I gave my word to Phoebe. It isn't as if P.C. Northcott is unaware of the murder. He is conducting his own investigation of the case and would no doubt resent my intrusion. Besides, all this is merely conjecture. I could be quite wrong in my assumptions."

"And if you are right?"

"Then I will inform the constable of my theory after the bishop has left."

His expression turned stony as he said, "I can see it's pointless to attempt to change your mind."

"Yes, Baxter," she said gently. "Quite pointless."

"Unfortunately I am not in a position to dictate what you should and should not do. There will come a time, however—"

He broke off, and Cecily felt her heart skip a beat. "Yes?" she said carefully. "You were about to say?"

"I was about to say that it's time I was on my way." He pushed back his chair and stood, then moved around to pull back her chair.

Frustrated, she rose, knowing it was futile to press him further. Once Baxter closed his mouth that way, nothing short of a team of horses would pry it open again.

"Would it be acceptable if I accompanied you to the church on Friday for the Clipping of the Church ceremony?" he inquired as she walked with him down the hallway to the lobby.

"I would like that very much." She waited while he retrieved his homburg from the hat stand, then added casually, "I would like to be there early so that I might have a chance to examine the chalice."

"I expected as much." His face looked forbidding in the shadows cast by the dim gas lamps. "I will be here at noon sharp. Since the service doesn't begin until two, that should give you plenty of time to conduct your investigation."

"Thank you, Baxter," Cecily said demurely. "I appreciate your understanding."

He looked at her suspiciously for a moment, then his expression softened. "I had hoped to discuss something of great importance with you tonight, Cecily. I can see that you have a great deal on your mind, however. I will wait until this matter is resolved, which, I assume, will be on Saturday. After that I shall have a short time in which to address my own concerns."

Once more she felt her heartbeat faltering. "Can you give me a hint as to what the discussion is about?"

He smiled. "I am afraid I must ask you to curb your impatience. For once I am in charge of the situation."

He kissed her hand before he left, leaving her in a state of seething curiosity and frustration. She wasn't used to this turnabout. It didn't sit well with her at all.

What made matters worse was the knowledge that there wasn't a thing that she could do about it. She would simply have to wait until Saturday to find out what it was that had Baxter behaving in such a peculiar manner.

In the meantime, she was faced with a formidable task. And this time she couldn't count on Baxter's help.

CHAPTER

❊ 13 ❊

"Have you gone to see madam about getting your job back, Ethel?" Gertie glanced at her friend, who sat at the table with a hot cup of tea in front of her. It seemed strange to see Ethel back in the kitchen of the Pennyfoot, almost as if she'd never gone away.

"Not yet. I was hoping to bump into her somewhere in the hotel." Ethel stirred her tea with a silver-crested teaspoon.

"You'll probably have to go up to her bloody suite and ask her," Gertie said, pouring tea into a cup for herself. "She's always bleeding flitting around so fast, you'll have a job to find her otherwise."

Ethel sighed. "I didn't want to sound that anxious about it."

"Why not? You are bleeding anxious, aren't you?" Gertie

carried her cup and saucer over to the table and sat down. "I thought you wanted to come back and flipping work here."

"I do. But it's not as if I can't get a job anywhere else. If madam thinks I'm that anxious to go back to work, she might tell me to go somewhere else."

"Not if you tell her you don't want to work for nobody else but her." Gertie sat back with a grin. "We had some bloody good times together, didn't we? Remember when the king was staying here and no one would believe it were really him?"

Ethel nodded. "Even you didn't believe me. You bet me sixpence I was wrong."

"Yeah. Then you made me knock on the flipping door to find out if it bleeding were him."

"And it were him, weren't it?"

"If it weren't, it were his bloody twin."

"Has he been back since?"

"Nah. Probably had enough of the two dopey housemaids what kept following him around."

Ethel stared dreamily into her teacup. "They were fun times."

"Yeah. A lot's happened since then." Gertie looked around as the door opened and Samuel bounded into the kitchen.

"Am I too late for me cuppa?" he asked, grinning at Ethel.

"Nah, I'll get it for you." Gertie got to her feet with a groan. "Cor blimey, me back's aching again. I'll be glad to get to bed tonight. I just hope me bloody twins don't wake up again."

Ethel sat up with a start. "Gawd, what's the time?" She looked over at the clock on the mantelpiece and gasped in dismay. "Is it that late? It will take me an hour to walk home. Joe will be wondering where on earth I got to."

"Don't worry, luv," Samuel said, taking the steaming cup from Gertie with a smile of thanks, "I'll run you home as soon as I've swallowed this."

"Oo, listen to him," Gertie said in a singsong voice. "The perfect bleeding gentleman. I'd bloody watch him, Ethel. He might be after something."

"I don't muck about with married women," Samuel said huffily. "I seen too many men get in trouble that way."

Ethel looked up at him and smiled. "Thank you, Samuel. I'd love a ride home. I don't fancy walking all that way in the dark. I might get thrown over the cliff like that poor Will Jones."

Gertie stared at her. "He was thrown over? I thought he bleeding fell on his own."

Ethel shrugged. "That's not what Nora Northcott told me."

"Go on. What were you doing talking to the flipping constable's wife?"

"She was in the doctor's office when I went in there for me cough. Ever since we moved to the Smoke, I got this awful cough."

"I know, I bleeding heard it." Gertie looked anxiously at her friend. She'd noticed that Ethel had no color in her cheeks anymore. "What did the doctor say?"

"He said as how it was a good job we moved out of London and come back to the fresh air. He says the sea air will do me good."

"What did Mrs. Northcott say about Will, then?" Samuel demanded, putting his empty cup back on the table.

"She says as how the police think Will was murdered by somebody. Hit on the head and pushed over the cliff, that's what they think."

Samuel shook his head. "Strewth. There was a lot of funny things going on that night. Someone borrowed one of the traps and brought it back all banged up. I hope it wasn't the murderer."

Ethel gave a start. "I thought I saw one of the Pennyfoot traps the night of the feast." She stared at Gertie, her eyes wide. "Remember I was going to come over here that night? Then I remembered about the feast, so I went for a walk instead, what with Joe being busy with the farm work. Well, it was on me way home. I knew it was a Pennyfoot trap because I saw the hotel sign on the side of it."

"Did you see who it was driving it?" Samuel asked.

"Nah. He had a cloth cap pulled low down on his head, didn't he? I couldn't see his face."

"Probably that bleeding twit Malcolm Ridlington," Gertie said in disgust. "I found him wandering around the cellars last night. Told me he was bleeding lost and couldn't find his way out."

"Well, it is really dark down there," Ethel said with a shudder. "I always hated going down there. All those passageways and doors. I'm surprised the guests don't get lost when they go down there."

Samuel laughed. "The only guests what go down there are the ones what are up to no good. They'd find their way out of hell if they had to."

"Well, I have to get going," Ethel said, looking at the clock again, "or I'll be catching hell from Joe."

"Come on, then." Samuel pulled his cap from his pocket and tugged it on. "I'll meet you out the front with the trap. You're lucky I haven't unharnessed it yet." He gave Gertie a cheerful wave and left.

"He's a nice young man," Ethel said, reaching for her wrap. "Make someone a good husband, he would."

"Don't bleeding look at me," Gertie said sharply. "He's too blooming young for me. Besides, I've bleeding had it with men."

"Oh?" Ethel gave her a sweet smile. "Is that why you're always talking about Ned Harris?"

"What, that cheeky bugger? I wouldn't give bleeding tuppence for him." Gertie sniffed and turned away, hoping Ethel wouldn't notice her warm cheeks.

"Not half, you wouldn't. Just give you the chance, that's all, and you'd be there."

"You'd better go," Gertie mumbled, "or you'll be bloody late."

Ethel laughed. "Night, night, then. I might be back tomorrow."

Gertie was glad to see her go for once. She didn't know why Ethel's flighty remarks bothered her so much. After all, Ned Harris meant nothing to her. Didn't he?

Crossing the lobby after saying good night to Baxter, Cecily was surprised to see Samuel bounding up the stairs from the kitchen. He halted when he saw her and pulled off his cap.

"Good evening, mum," he mumbled, twisting the cap in his hands.

"Good evening, Samuel." Cecily watched him, wondering what mischief he'd been up to that would put that look of guilt on his face.

"I was wondering, mum," Samuel said, throwing a glance back over his shoulder, "would it be all right if I run Ethel home before I put the trap away? It won't take more than a few minutes."

Cecily smiled. "Ethel? She's here? You are referring to the Ethel who worked here, aren't you?"

"Oh, yes, mum," Samuel said, vigorously nodding his head. "She's been up here a couple of times to visit Gertie. I was going to tell you tomorrow, 'cause she saw something I thought you might want to know about."

Cecily's attention sharpened. "She saw something?"

"Yes, mum. She saw one of our traps driving away from the church on Monday night. I think it might be the one what got borrowed the other night."

"I see," Cecily said slowly. "Did she happen to see who was driving it?"

Samuel started to shake his head, then turned it when footsteps sounded on the stairs. "Here she is now, mum. You can ask her yourself. I'd better go and get the trap."

Cecily nodded. "Thank you, Samuel. Don't be back late."

"No, mum. I won't, honest." Samuel touched his forehead, then dashed off, just as Ethel reached the top of the stairs.

She dropped a curtsey at once. "Good evening, mum. It's a pleasure to see you again, I'm sure."

"It's a pleasure for me also, Ethel." Cecily smiled at the young woman with genuine affection. "How long will you be in Badgers End?"

"Oh, we're living down here again, mum. Didn't no one tell you?"

"No one mentioned it to me. Is Joe with you?"

"Well, he's at home, mum. Bought hisself a farm on the other side of the Downs. I just came up to see Gertie's babies."

"Yes, they're quite a handful, I imagine." Cecily glanced around, but they seemed to be quite alone. Ned had gone off duty, and most of the guests were either retired for the night or playing cards down in the cellars.

"Samuel tells me you saw one of our traps drive away from the church the other night," she said quietly.

Ethel nodded. "Yes, mum. I saw the hotel sign on the side of it."

"You didn't see who was driving it?"

"No, mum, I didn't. I thought it might be someone what forgot there was no service that night."

"Yes, I'm sure that's what it was. It's just that we like to know when someone takes one of our traps out. I prefer that Samuel or one of the footmen drive them."

"Yes, mum, I know." Ethel looked as if she wanted to run away. She dithered for a moment or two while Cecily waited, wondering what was on the girl's mind.

Finally, when Ethel seemed as if she would stand there tongue-tied forever, Cecily asked gently, "Is there something else you want to tell me?"

Ethel shook her head. "Not tell you, exactly mum. More like ask you." She paused, then brought the next words out in a rush. "I was wondering if I could have me old job back. Mrs. Chubb is always saying as how she could use another pair of hands, and I thought maybe I could come back here." She let out her breath in a rush, as if she'd been holding it back until then.

Pleasantly surprised at the request, Cecily took a moment to answer her. "I'd be delighted to have you back at the Pennyfoot," she said at last, "but I really don't know if we can manage another wage right now. We have taken on a doorman, and I don't think we'll have enough left over to afford another housemaid."

Ethel looked so disappointed that Cecily wished desperately she could have taken the girl back right then and there.

"That's all right, mum," Ethel said mournfully. "I just thought I'd ask, seeing as how I always enjoyed working here so much, like."

"I'll ask my manager about it," Cecily promised, without much hope. "Maybe we can work something out."

"Oh, thank you, mum, I'd be ever so obliged if you could have me back."

"I can't promise anything," Cecily warned, "but I'll discuss it with Mr. Ridlington first thing in the morning."

She watched Ethel leave, wishing that she felt more

optimistic about her new manager's answer. If it had been Baxter, he might have been willing to investigate the possibility. Malcolm Ridlington was a different proposition altogether.

Her assessment of the dour manager proved to be right the next morning when she faced him across his desk in the tiny office that still vibrated with memories of Baxter.

"Hire another housemaid?" he muttered when Cecily gave him her request. "I'd like to know, madam, where are we going to find the money for that?"

"Perhaps we can cut down somewhere else," Cecily suggested.

"We are cut to the bare bones as it is, madam. Look for yourself." He picked up a sheaf of papers and handed them to her.

Cecily skimmed down the untidy lists with a frown. They seemed unnecessarily haphazard, and there were several items that she didn't understand.

"What does this mean?" she asked, pointing to an entry marked under housekeeping. "Fifty pounds for stable supplies? What did we need for the stables that cost fifty pounds?"

"That's feed, madam," Malcolm said pompously. "We do need to feed the horses, I presume."

His attitude was beginning to annoy her. "The entry should be under maintenance," she said evenly. "And I doubt that we spend fifty pounds on an entire year of feed. This bill should be closer to fifteen pounds."

"Let me look." He took the list from her and studied it. "Perhaps you're right, madam. I'll look into it."

"Please do. And while you are about it, also look into the figures you have down for the work on the plumbing. I'm sure we were charged more than a shilling an hour."

Malcolm's fuzzy brows drew together in a frown. "Yes, of course . . . I can't imagine . . . I'll take care of it."

Cecily studied his grim face for a moment. "Malcolm," she said quietly, "if you are having trouble with this work, I do wish you would let Mr. Baxter help while he is here. I'm quite sure he—"

"Thank you, madam. As I've said before, most emphatically, I do not need Mr. Baxter's assistance or anyone else's for that matter. I can assure you I am quite capable of handling everything myself. All I need is a little time to make sense of the chaos left behind by your Mr. Baxter."

"My chaos, Malcolm. Not Mr. Baxter's."

"That's as may be, madam. The fact remains that there is still work to be done on these books. As for this business of hiring a new housemaid, I suggest we drop the matter. It is my contention that if things are allowed to continue the way they have been, not only will we not be able to afford more staff, but also we shall most likely be forced to get rid of some of those we already have."

Cecily stared at him in dismay. "Things cannot be that bad, Malcolm. After all, we are having the best summer season we've ever had. The hotel has been full practically every week since Easter."

"We have also been quite lavish with our services. The catering bills are quite horrendous. Extravagant in my opinion, if I might say so."

"We demand a high price for the rooms. We must provide the kind of service to which the aristocrats are accustomed. That is why we can fill our hotel with high-paying guests."

Malcolm scowled at his ledger. "I didn't notice the women's bicycle club paying a particularly high price, madam."

"That is because there were so many of them. It has

always been our policy, set by my late husband many years ago, that a large group would pay less."

"And receive the same service."

"For which the hotel is renowned."

"It is an odd way to do business, madam. No wonder there are problems with the finances."

"Well, do the best you can," Cecily said shortly. "I suppose you will not be at the clipping service tomorrow?"

He looked up and gave her a look that came close to insolence. "I shall be chained to my desk, as usual, madam."

Cecily left then, before she gave in to the urge to tell him exactly what she thought of him. Aware that some of her resentment stemmed from the fact that he was not Baxter, which was hardly his fault, she nevertheless couldn't help feeling that in this case at least, Baxter was right. Perhaps she had, indeed, made a very bad mistake in hiring Malcolm Ridlington.

Reaching the lobby, she looked across at her other new employee, Ned Harris. To her surprise, he was holding an animated conversation with Gertie. The housemaid seemed to be quite enjoying his remarks, judging from her flushed cheeks and the way she tossed her head in a flirtatious manner when she answered him.

Catching Cecily's eye, Ned touched the peak of his cap. "Morning, mum. Looks like the rain has stopped. Must be Saint Bartholomew clearing the skies for his ceremony tomorrow, shouldn't wonder."

"Could be, indeed, Ned."

Gertie dropped a hasty curtsey and turned to go.

"Just a moment, Gertie." Cecily approached the confused-looking housemaid and added, "When you see Ethel, please tell her that I'm sorry. Mr. Ridlington doesn't think we can manage another housemaid at the present. Please tell her that we'll keep her in mind, however, should we have an opening later on."

"Yes, mum, I'll tell her. Thank you, mum."

"How are my godchildren doing? I haven't had much chance to see them lately, since we've been so busy."

"They are doing very well, mum. Thank you. Every time I look at them, they seem to get bleeding bigger."

Cecily laughed. "Mr. Baxter mentioned that he'd like to see the twins before he returns to London, since he is their godfather. I believe he has a present for them. I'll bring him down to the kitchen. I know he'll want to see everyone before he leaves."

"That would be very nice, mum."

"You are going to the clipping service tomorrow? I know Mrs. Carter-Holmes is counting on everyone being there."

"Yes, mum." Gertie gave Ned a sidelong glance. "Me and Ned are going together. He's going to give me a hand with the twins."

Cecily looked at Ned in surprise. She really couldn't imagine her doorman dealing with two active babies.

Ned grinned back at her. "Used to have two of me own, I did. I was just telling Gertie about them."

"I didn't know you were married, Ned," Cecily said, wondering why he hadn't mentioned it before.

"Well, I don't like to talk about it much." Ned and Gertie exchanged glances, as if they were sharing a secret. "Anyhow, I'm not married now, and that's what counts, I reckon."

"Well, I'll see you both at the church, then," Cecily said, feeling as if she'd just been shut out. She glanced at the clock as she crossed the lobby again. She didn't have time to wonder about Ned and his mysterious past right now. There was something urgent that she had to do.

Three people were absent from the feast on Monday

night. According to Malcolm Ridlington, he was in the
office for the entire evening, working on the accounts. That
left Primrose Parsons and Sid Barker, and Cecily wanted
very much to talk to both of them.

Someone, presumably from the hotel, had taken out a trap
the night Will Jones was murdered. Cecily wanted to know
exactly where her two guests had spent the evening. She
could only hope that they both had a satisfactory answer.

CHAPTER
❖ 14 ❖

Cecily found Primrose Parsons in the drawing room, enjoying a cup of tea with several of her companions. All the women were fashionably dressed in the shorter, full skirts that most lady cyclists now wore.

The display of so many trim ankles had apparently attracted the attention of Colonel Fortescue, who stood in the middle of the room, fruitlessly attempting to engage some of the women in conversation.

"Prefer horses myself," the colonel trumpeted, twirling the waxed ends of his luxuriant mustache with his fingers. "They know when to stop, by George. Those infernal bicycle machines can run away with you if you don't watch out. I remember when I was in India—"

Some of the unfortunate women happened to be too close

157

to the colonel to politely ignore him. Seeing their dazed expressions, Cecily hurried forward. "Good morning, Colonel," she said loudly. "Ladies? I do hope everything is to your satisfaction?"

"Quite, quite," the women murmured, more than one sending an indignant glance at the colonel.

"Oh, good morning, old bean," he bellowed at Cecily. "Jolly good to see you, what?"

"I was wondering, Colonel," Cecily said, giving him a sweet smile, "if you would assist me in a small problem. My bartender tells me that the bottle of gin he opened yesterday didn't seem quite up to par. Would you mind going down there to taste it for me? Tell him I sent you, and I'll speak to him about it later this afternoon."

The colonel's eyes lit up like Christmas candles. "By Jove, madam, I'll be only too happy to oblige. Yes, indeed. You can rely on me, old girl. Won't let you down." He rushed from the room, and the ladies uttered audible sighs of relief.

"Thank goodness that dreadful man has gone," Primrose Parsons said, dabbing the end of her pointed nose with her handkerchief. "He was upsetting my stomach quite badly with his awful stories." She gave Cecily an accusing look. "I have a weak stomach, you know."

Cecily gave her a sympathetic smile. "Actually, Miss Parsons, that is why I am here. I came to inquire after your health. I hope the light menu I recommended for your stomach has helped ease the problem?"

The woman gave a reluctant nod. "It has, Mrs. Sinclair. I am much obliged."

"I would not wish for you to miss another meal," Cecily said carefully. "I regret that you could not enjoy the feast of Saint Bartholomew the other night. It was such a shame that you had to spend the entire evening in your room."

Primrose Parsons gave her a long, intent look. "It was indeed, Mrs. Sinclair. As you can see, however, I have recovered."

"Why didn't you tell us you were ill that night?" one of the women exclaimed. "We would have been happy to bring you something to eat and sit with you."

Primrose Parsons lifted her chin. "Mrs. Sinclair was kind enough to send a light meal up to my room," she said shortly. "After which I lay down on my bed. I much prefer to be alone when I'm not feeling well. There are times when peace and quiet can be the best medicine."

The women looked affronted at this curt comment, but no one said anything.

"Well," Cecily said, sending a smile around the group, "I'm happy to see that you have recovered. If anyone should need anything, please don't hesitate to ask one of the staff. We are all ready and willing to help in any way we can." Amid a chorus of polite thanks, she left the room.

Sid Barker was harder to find. He wasn't in his room, nor did he appear to be anywhere in the hotel. Hoping he hadn't left for the day, Cecily went to ask Ned if he'd seen him.

"Went out the door about half an hour ago," Ned informed her. "I saw him with me own minces."

Cecily gave him a questioning look. "Minces?"

"Mince pies." Ned tapped his eyebrow.

"Eyes," Cecily said with a sigh.

Ned shrugged. "Sorry, mum. Hard to break the habit, it is."

"Yes, well, please do your best." Cecily stepped out onto the porch. "Did you happen to see Mr. Sid Barker leave the hotel?"

"Yes, mum, I did. He was making for the tennis courts, though I don't think he was going to play. I didn't see a bat in his hand."

"A racquet, Ned."

"Pardon, mum?"

"It's a tennis racquet, not a bat."

"Yes, mum. Whatever you say."

Sighing, Cecily started down the steps. As she did so, she saw the bishop hurrying up toward them, looking quite flustered. He answered her greeting with a frantic flap of his hand, seemed as if he would rush by her, then apparently thought better of it and paused in front of her.

"Good morning, Mrs. Sinclair. I was just getting a breath of fresh air. Nice morning for it."

Cecily looked toward the ocean. "It is, indeed, Bishop. The sea still looks gray, however. I do believe we shall have more rain before the day is out."

"Really? I hope it clears up by tomorrow, then." He looked hopefully at Cecily. "Though I suppose the vicar will cancel the ceremony if it's wet?"

"I rather doubt it." Cecily smiled at the thought of Phoebe giving up on anything she'd organized.

"I did think he might cancel the ceremony after that poor fellow died. Bell ringer, wasn't he? Doesn't seem quite right to celebrate when one of the church members has so recently passed away."

"Will Jones would have wanted the ceremony to continue," Cecily said quietly. "He was dedicated to the church."

"Oh, quite, quite." The bishop shook his head. "Dreadful accident, that. That path must be most treacherous if one can fall over the cliffs so easily. Makes one fear for the children, doesn't it? A path like that should be prohibited to the public, in my opinion. Pretty poor management by the town, that's what I say."

Stung by his criticism, Cecily lifted her chin. "The path is perfectly safe, Bishop, as long as one keeps to it. As a matter of fact, Will Jones did not fall to his death. The police believe he was killed and then pushed over the cliff."

"K-killed? Oh, my dear Lord." The bishop looked as if he'd been struck by lightning. He seemed to freeze for a second or two, swallowed several times, then turned his head this way and that as if looking for someone. "I can't believe . . . that poor man . . ."

"Are you all right, Bishop?" Cecily asked, wishing she hadn't allowed herself to be provoked. She hadn't meant to be so indiscreet.

"What?" He looked at her, his face drawn with shock. "Oh, yes, quite. It's just . . . I've never been this close to murder before. It's quite horrifying. One doesn't expect . . . in such a tranquil setting . . ." He seemed to collect himself with an effort. "Do the police know who perpetrated this most heinous act?"

"Not as yet, to my knowledge," Cecily said, concerned now by her imprudence. "I do hope you will keep this to yourself, Bishop. While I'm sure there is no immediate danger, it wouldn't do to alarm our guests."

He gave her an anxious look. "Of course not. You can count on me to keep it under my hat." He shivered, though the air was quite warm. "Dreadful business, murder. Absolutely dreadful." He turned away and continued up the steps, muttering quietly to himself.

He was going to feel a good deal worse by Saturday, Cecily thought, if the chalice had not been retrieved by then. Feeling guilty about keeping such momentous news from the bishop, she hurried down the steps and across the well-kept lawns to the tennis courts.

Sid Barker lounged against a tree, his hands in his pockets, watching with apparent boredom an energetic foursome smashing a ball across the nets.

The steady pock of the racquets hitting the ball was

punctured by good-natured remarks from the two men, while the women preserved their breath and hopped about the grass court as daintily as their long skirts would allow.

After exchanging a greeting with Sid Barker, Cecily paused at his side, pretending an interest in watching the game. "Do you play tennis, Mr. Barker?" she asked as the couples changed ends.

He shook his head. "Never tried it."

"Neither have I, but it does look like fun. I'm not sure I have the energy, though."

He didn't answer, and she tried again. "We missed you at the feast the other night. I do hope you weren't ill?"

This time she had his attention. He swiveled his head to look at her, and though his expression was bland enough, his eyes were wary. "I was there," he said with a note of belligerence in his voice. "I came in a little late, that was all. I fell asleep in my room after that exhausting ride and didn't wake up until after the meal had begun."

Confused, Cecily stared at him. She couldn't remember exactly when she looked for him in the dining room. He could have come in late, of course, though she was sure she would have noticed if he had. Then again, she had been rather preoccupied with Baxter.

Sid Barker was still watching her with that odd wariness in his eyes. She managed a smile and said evenly, "I'm happy you were able to join us after all. I do hope you enjoyed the meal?"

"I did. The lobster and roast beef were excellent."

"Thank you. We are very proud of our chef."

He didn't answer but stood there waiting as if he wanted to leave and wasn't sure how to go about it.

"Well," Cecily said, "I'll leave you to enjoy the game. I must get back to my duties."

He gave her a polite nod, then turned back to the courts.

Cecily left him there and walked slowly back across the grass to the hotel, still unconvinced. Sid Barker's answers had seemed just a little too pat.

Or was she reading too much into them perhaps? It could be that she was just a little too anxious to find the killer and was jumping at every possibility, no matter how remote.

It would seem that she was back where she had started, and time was running out. Poor Algie would have to face the music on Saturday after all. Worse, it was entirely possible that Will's murderer might go free.

If the culprit was a guest at the hotel, as Cecily believed, he would be forced to stay the entire week as booked. To leave earlier was bound to raise suspicion. By Sunday morning, however, everyone would be leaving, thereby giving the murderer the opportunity to escape undetected.

That was not a comforting thought.

Cecily's prediction of more rain proved correct. By nightfall the showers were quite heavy, washing down the windows and rushing along the gutters of the Pennyfoot's red roofs.

Cecily talked to several members of her staff, but no one could remember seeing Sid Barker in the dining room the night of the feast. Then again, no one could say definitely that he wasn't there.

The staff had been rushed off their feet, scurrying back and forth between kitchen and dining room all night. With the hotel full to capacity and everyone attending the feast, there had been no time to take note of whom they were serving.

By the time Cecily retired for the night, the rain had once more ceased, leaving behind the fragrance of damp grass and dewy blossoms in the salty night air.

She stood for a moment at the window, trying to calm her troubled thoughts. She was convinced now that the theft of the chalice and Will's death were connected. Baxter was right; she should have informed the constable. It seemed unlikely that Northcott was close to a solution.

She was not about to share her conviction that the killer was a guest, however. Much as she wanted the murderer caught, her first priority was to protect the hotel.

The Pennyfoot had a reputation to uphold, one that promised complete privacy and seclusion for its aristocratic guests. While the members of the women's bicycle club were not in that class, word of any intrusion by the constabulary could easily leak out in London's more affluent circles.

Allowing the constable—or worse, Inspector Cranshaw—to tramp around the hotel questioning everybody was to invite more trouble.

No, Cecily told herself. She was doing the right thing by keeping quiet about the chalice, at least until she'd had the chance to investigate further. She should have that chance tomorrow at the church, though she wasn't sure what more she could do.

Her instincts told her that Sid Barker was somehow involved. Yet she would need more proof than feminine intuition. Somehow she had to find that proof, even if it meant searching his room.

In fact, she decided, that's exactly what she would do. At the very next opportunity that offered itself. Most likely it would be the following afternoon, after she returned from the church. That would give her a chance to ask Baxter for his help. For no matter how much he protested, she was certain that if he thought she would be in danger, he would not be able to refuse.

If she found the chalice in Sid Barker's room, as she expected to, she would hand it over to the constable, together with her theory, and let him take things from there.

Feeling a great deal better, she made ready for bed, excited now at the thought of seeing Baxter again. She had missed him throughout that long day. It was a small measure of how much she would miss him once he went back to London. Unless her instincts had been right about him wanting to court her.

Her heart fluttered at the very thought of it. Just how far she could trust her instincts, she wasn't certain. It would be better not to dwell on it, for she knew now that if she was wrong about his intentions, the disappointment would be devastating.

She fell into an uneasy sleep and awoke to the sound of the songbirds greeting the morning from the branches of the ancient yew that grew outside her window.

The morning seemed to drag by, until at last it was almost noon and she was dressed and waiting for Baxter. He arrived promptly at noon and escorted her down the steps of the Pennyfoot with a hand under her arm.

Samuel was waiting with the trap at the foot of the steps. The Pennyfoot's staff would be walking to the church for the clipping, though most of them would have to return afterward without attending the service in order to have the meal ready when the rest of the guests returned.

The majority of the guests planned to ride their bicycles to the church, for which Samuel was extremely grateful. Otherwise he would have been hard pushed to transport everyone there in the traps.

Since the ceremony wasn't to take place until two, only the members of the dance troupe were at the church when Baxter and Cecily arrived. The girls were dashing about here and there, seemingly without any trace of organization.

"This doesn't seem a good time to examine the chalice," Cecily murmured regretfully. "I was rather hoping we'd have the church to ourselves. I suppose it will have to wait until after the ceremony, when everyone has left."

"How those reprehensible young women expect to herd a hundred people into some semblance of order I can't imagine," Baxter said as he stood with Cecily watching the chaos. "They can't even keep themselves under restraint."

A loud shriek from one of the girls echoed chillingly through the rafters. Almost immediately a squabble broke out, with several of the dancers talking and gesturing at once.

"I wonder where Phoebe is," Cecily murmured. "I'm surprised she's not in here taking charge of the situation."

"Most likely staying out of the fray until the last possible moment, if she has any sense."

Cecily smiled up at him. "You sound a little liverish this morning, Baxter. Did you not sleep well?"

"I haven't slept well since I arrived in Badgers End." He avoided her gaze and kept his eyes fixed on the bickering girls. "It must be the noise from the barrooms below that disturbs me."

"The pub closes at eleven o'clock most nights," Cecily pointed out.

Baxter cleared his throat. "Yes, well, I have a lot on my mind. Your insistence on tracking down a murderer, for example. I suppose it is futile to hope you have given up on the idea by now?"

"On the contrary, Baxter, I think I have the matter solved. I shall need your assistance, however. I really don't want to do this alone."

He looked down at her then, his face full of suspicion. "Now what would you have me do?"

Again the shrieks rang out. She put her hand on his arm and led him outside. "I will tell you on the way back to the hotel," she told him. "For now I think we had better find

Phoebe and let her know that her charges are about to destroy the church."

They walked together down the path that led to the vicarage, their feet crunching on the damp gravel. "Thank goodness the rain has stopped," Cecily said as they turned the corner of the church. "It really would have—" She broke off, brought to a halt by the sight of Phoebe and Algie in the graveyard.

They stood side by side, saying nothing, staring down at the ground in front of them. Something about their still, intent manner gave Cecily a chill.

"I wonder what it is that holds their attention so raptly," she said to Baxter. Hitching up the skirt of her light gray suit, she made her way across the moist grass, with Baxter following close behind.

Phoebe looked up as they approached. Beneath the brim of her hat her cheeks looked pale and her eyes wide. "Oh, Cecily," she said, "there you are. And Mr. Baxter, how good to see you."

Baxter touched the brim of his homburg. "It is a pleasure as always, Mrs. Carter-Holmes." He looked at Algie. "Vicar?"

Algie gave him a distracted nod. "Good day, Mrs. Sinclair, Mr. Baxter."

"Do you have any news for us, Cecily?" Phoebe asked urgently.

Cecily shook her head. "I'm afraid not yet, though I haven't given up on the puzzle." She glanced at Algie, who seemed mesmerized by the mound of earth at his feet. "Is something wrong?" she asked him, watching him with a growing certainty that something was very wrong indeed.

Phoebe lifted her hands in a little gesture of helplessness. "We really don't know, as yet. It seems that we have discovered a new grave."

Baxter uttered a brief exclamation, while Cecily frowned. "A new grave?"

"Yes." Phoebe looked back at the freshly dug mound of earth. "Algie noticed it because it wasn't in line with the others. That's when he took a closer look at it."

"Are you certain it's a fresh grave?" Cecily asked. "Could you simply not have noticed it was out of line before?"

"That space was reserved for Nathan Puckett's wife," Phoebe said, her voice fading. "She was here yesterday morning, laying fresh flowers on her husband's grave." She pointed to a small vase of chrysanthemums on the next grave. "I spoke to her myself. And I'm quite certain there was no grave there yesterday."

She looked back at Cecily, her eyes wide with apprehension. "The question is who do you suppose is lying in it?"

CHAPTER

❧ 15 ❧

For a long moment, all four people stared down at the mound of earth that had now taken on an ominous appearance. "What are we going to do?" Phoebe whispered, twisting her handkerchief tightly in her gloved hands.

"I suppose we should dig it up," Algie said, his voice wavering. "Otherwise, how are we to know who is ah . . . buried there?"

Phoebe gave a loud moan and swayed against Cecily. "Oh, my, I think I'm going to have one of my turns."

Cecily took hold of her arm. "We don't have time for that, Phoebe. We must consider what is best to be done."

"I should think that is quite obvious," Baxter said. "We must inform the constable at once."

Algie gave a faint cry. "No, no, we can't do that. The b-bishop will be arriving soon."

"Not to mention a hundred people," Cecily murmured, giving Baxter a warning look.

"But if someone is buried there . . ."

Phoebe gave another loud moan. "What are we going to do? All those people . . ."

"I really don't think we can do . . . ah . . . anything until after the service," Algie said, looking hopefully at Cecily. "P.C. Northcott will be at the service. Can't we . . . ah . . . tell him then? After everyone has gone home?"

Especially the bishop, Cecily thought, feeling a certain sympathy for Algie. He was terrified that the man would find out the chalice had been stolen.

"I really don't think we should wait that long," Baxter said, giving Cecily a meaningful frown.

"I think the vicar is right," she said firmly. "After all, can you imagine the pandemonium we would have if a hundred people were here to watch the constable dig up the grave? We must keep quiet about this until after the service." She looked back at the sinister mound of earth. "After all," she added, "it's not as if whoever is in it is going anywhere."

"I feel faint," Phoebe moaned. "I don't think I can manage to walk back to the church."

"You must," Cecily urged, patting her arm. "Your dancers need you. At the moment they are squabbling amongst themselves inside the church. I'm afraid they might do some damage."

"Oh, my," Phoebe said breathlessly, "those dreadful girls. They are supposed to be outside getting everyone into position. I had better run over there and restore order at once."

She hurried off, leaving Algie staring after her. "I do hope she doesn't say anything," he muttered. "Mother has always had trouble holding her tongue. If the b-bishop should discover that the chalice has been stolen, my life will be ruined." He gave a horrified gasp and slapped his hand over his mouth, staring wide-eyed at Baxter.

"Please don't concern yourself," Cecily said quickly. "I have enlisted Mr. Baxter's help. He will not mention the theft to anyone, and I'm sure your mother will be far too busy to say anything either."

"Yes, well, I hope you are right." He uttered a long sigh. "It is fortunate the rain has stopped. Had it not, we would have had to hold the service inside the church. I only hope that the b-bishop doesn't decide to go inside to inspect the chalice." Hitching up his cassock, he rushed off after Phoebe.

"I don't care for this situation," Baxter said, eyeing the mound of earth. "I don't care for it one little bit."

"I don't either," Cecily assured him. "I'm assuming we shall find another victim under that mound."

"Well, at least this time you have consented to inform the constable."

Cecily gave him a look of pure innocence. "Why, Baxter, I would never keep such important information from the authorities. You know me better than that."

"Which is precisely why I still feel uneasy," Baxter said, looking morose. "Something tells me this new development could well lead you further into danger."

"Piffle. You worry too much." She felt most comforted to know that he still worried about her, but she wasn't about to admit as much. Leaving his side, she paced slowly around the new grave, inspecting the ground very carefully, all the time aware of his intent gaze on her.

There appeared to be an interesting pattern of footsteps left in the rain-softened earth. One set in particular caught her attention. The sole was a long oval, together with a deep indent for the heel.

She paused for a long moment at the head of the grave, studying the footprints, then she returned to his side. "Well, shall we go and join in the festivities? Phoebe should have the dance troupe in hand by now."

"If that's at all possible," Baxter said, taking her arm. "Personally, I shall be quite amazed if those barbarians can manage anything short of total bedlam."

"Then let us hope they surprise us both," Cecily said serenely. She was rather looking forward to dancing around the church with Baxter, and she really wasn't too concerned about how well it was organized.

She didn't know how much more time she would spend in his company, and she was determined to make the most of it. For once, even the pursuit of a murderer paled in significance.

A large number of people had arrived by the time Cecily and Baxter reached the church. Phoebe was flying about, shouting commands to her dance troupe, most of which were blithely ignored.

A little girl in a pure white pinafore and flowing golden locks pranced around, handing out song sheets, which, Cecily discovered, had the words to the song everyone was supposed to sing.

Baxter stared at his sheet in disgust. "How the devil are we supposed to sing a song when we've never heard the tune?" he demanded of no one in particular.

"We follow everyone else," Cecily said, trying not to laugh at the offended expression on his face. "Actually, Baxter, the prospect of hearing you sing for the first time has me breathless with anticipation."

"Really." He gave her a cynical look. "I suggest you curb

your excitement. My voice has been likened to that of a mountain goat."

She laughed. "Then we shall make a good pair, no doubt."

Her laughter died when she caught sight of the intent expression in his eyes. "Indeed we shall," he said solemnly.

Before she could fully recover, a hefty young woman, whom Cecily recognized as one of Phoebe's dance troupe, pounced on her and took hold of her hand. "Here you go, ma'am," she boomed, "hold onto this gentleman's hand and wait here until I give the signal."

Cecily didn't know quite where to look. Somehow, standing there with her hand in Baxter's firm grip seemed so decadent. Judging by the stoic expression on his face, he was no more comfortable with the situation than she was. He stood staring straight ahead, refusing to look at her.

After a moment or two, however, Cecily relaxed. Stretching out in a long line that reached around the corner of the church, everyone there held the hand of the person next to them.

In fact, Baxter's look of intense discomfort could have been caused by the fact that his other hand was clamped in the grasp of a burly farmer, who was doing his best to engage his new friend in animated conversation.

Before long the other end of the human chain came into view around the opposite corner of the church. Cecily saw Kevin Prestwick, deep in conversation with a matronly woman who kept hiding girlish giggles behind a fan.

A shy young girl was the last to be joined, and then the tubby dancer grasped Cecily's free hand. "All right," the young woman bellowed in a voice that could well have been heard at the other end of the village, "we're all joined up."

Phoebe flew around the corner, clutching her hat. "Well done, everybody," she cried, gasping for breath. "The girls will sing the song through once for you, so that you can hear the tune. Then everyone will start singing. We might not all start at once, but I'm hoping we shall all catch up with one another by the time we've circled the church. Just follow the person in front and do what he or she does. Now, everybody, turn to the left, if you please."

Cecily obediently turned toward Marion, who turned to face her. "I think she said left," Cecily murmured.

"Oh, blimey, I never remember which is which," Marion muttered. She turned around and started singing in a high-pitched, tuneless voice that made Cecily wince. Phoebe had now disappeared, apparently to issue the same instructions to the rest of the line.

Marion came to the end of the verse, then bellowed, "All right, everybody, follow me."

Conscious of Baxter right behind her, his hand grasping hers with a deathlike grip, Cecily did her best to sing the unfamiliar song and follow Marion's somewhat erratic sidesteps.

Ahead of Marion the line was lurching from side to side as the rest of the dance troupe urged their charges forward. Cecily caught sight of Gertie, whose hand was in that of Ned Harris. Farther up the line, Doris and Daisy danced behind Mrs. Chubb, looking as if they were having the time of their lives. Cecily wondered who was taking care of the babies.

The noise was deafening as everyone sang as loud as possible to drown out everyone else who wasn't in tune. Gradually, as they clumsily circled the church with much stumbling and tripping, everyone found the melody, and the last chorus of the song rang out with gusto.

Behind her Cecily heard Baxter singing in a pleasant baritone, and without warning tears stung her eyes. As chaotic as it was, the sound of a hundred people joined by the hand and all singing in unison, with the notes echoing across the ancient roof of the church, moved her deeply.

She was apparently not the only one to be affected, as when the line came to a halt and the hands were dropped, several of the women surreptitiously dabbed at their eyes with a handkerchief.

Phoebe herself, sniffing audibly, helped her dance troupe usher the congregation onto the front lawn, where chairs had been set up for the service. The bishop, resplendent in a crimson chasuble and miter, took his place at the right of the podium, and Algie, looking as if he would faint dead away from fright at any second, mounted the steps to address the congregation.

Seated next to Baxter, Cecily murmured, "That was quite entertaining. It seems as if everyone enjoyed the ceremony."

Baxter uttered a disparaging grunt. "Somewhat asinine, in my opinion. All that ridiculous prancing about."

"Really? I thought you rather enjoyed the singing part. You certainly sounded as if you did."

Baxter cleared his throat. "I see Prestwick is here, charming the ladies as usual. I'm surprised he hasn't made a beeline for you. He's not usually so remiss."

"I doubt that he's had time," Cecily said, glancing across to where the doctor sat between two fawning women. "He's been surrounded by admirers ever since he arrived."

"I can't for the life of me imagine why."

Neither could Cecily, but she wasn't about to give Baxter that satisfaction. "I'm so happy for Phoebe," she said, changing the subject. "Everything went wonderfully well for a change."

"Don't speak too soon," Baxter muttered. "It looks as if we might lose our vicar at any second."

Algie somehow managed to pull himself together, however, and delivered the service in his monotonous voice that left his audience feeling thoroughly restless by the time it was over.

Noticing one or two people furtively leaving, Cecily kept her eye on P.C. Northcott, who appeared to be dozing in his chair on the edge of the crowd. Finally it was over. Algie leapt down the steps as the bishop got slowly to his feet.

Cecily saw the constable moving away and turned to Baxter. "We must try to detain P.C. Northcott until after everyone has left. Then we can tell him about the fresh grave."

Baxter looked down his nose at her. "If we must."

Cecily sighed. "I'm sorry, Baxter. I know you detest the man, but we can't let him leave."

"More's the pity." Scowling, Baxter followed her to where the constable stood talking to the bishop. Algie hovered nearby, sending frightened little glances back at the church every now and again. Phoebe was nowhere to be seen.

As Cecily approached, the bishop broke off his conversation and greeted her. Cecily introduced Baxter, while Algie continued to hop about like a frightened rabbit.

Feeling sorry for the vicar, Cecily said to the bishop, "I saw Samuel waiting out by the gate. I imagine he is waiting to take you back to the hotel."

"Oh, right, yes," the bishop said, looking over there. "I asked him to wait for me. I don't like to walk that far in these clothes. Attracts too much attention, you know."

"Yes, I imagine it does." Cecily smiled up at him. "I'm sure Samuel is happy to drive you back to the Pennyfoot."

"Yes, quite. Well, I'll be off, then." The bishop turned to Algie, who started violently. "Jolly good service there, Vicar. I enjoyed the clipping ceremony very much. Nice touch, that."

Algie's face turned bright red. "Th-thank you, B-bishop."

"Yes, well, see you tomorrow, then, right? Have to get that chalice back to its proper home again, you know."

Algie made a little squeaking sound.

"I will see you in the dining room tonight, then, Bishop," Cecily said firmly.

The bishop looked at her. "What? Oh, yes. Of course. Until then, Mrs. Sinclair." He nodded at Baxter and P.C. Northcott, then strode off, looking a little like an oversized penguin strutting down the path.

"Where is Phoebe?" Cecily asked Algie, who stood fanning his red face with the copy of his sermon.

Phoebe answered for him, as she rounded the corner of the church just then. "The girls are going to carry the chairs back into the church hall for us," she said, giving Cecily a direct stare. Her head inclined just slightly toward the graveyard.

"Well, I must be off, too," the constable announced. "Got me duties to attend to, I do. Can't stand around here talking all day."

"Er, Constable," Cecily said before Northcott could move, "I wonder if we might have a word with you?"

Northcott looked at her suspiciously. "Not about the death of Will Jones, I hope, Mrs. Sinclair? You know I can't discuss the matter with you. The h'inspector would not like that. Not at all."

"I suppose there have been no further developments in the case?" Cecily said hopefully.

Northcott heaved an exaggerated sigh. "Even if there was, Mrs. Sinclair, I could not discuss it with you. Now if you'll excuse me—"

Algie looked anxiously at Cecily, while Phoebe looked ready to burst. At that moment, the entire dance troupe charged around the corner, laughing uproariously. Each of them grabbed up a chair and began to carry them off.

They had not gone far, however, before one of the girls tripped over the legs of her companion's chair.

"You blooming done that on purpose," the girl's strident voice declared.

"Did not," the other girl said indignantly. "It's not my fault if you can't blinking look where you're going."

"Perhaps we should go inside the church," Cecily said hastily.

The constable shook his head. "Look, Mrs. Sinclair, with all due respect, I really don't have time to listen to gossip. I have me duties waiting for me down at the station."

More like a cup of tea and a copy of the local newspaper, Cecily thought.

"Don't be such an oaf, Northcott," Baxter said suddenly. "You can at least hear the lady out."

The constable's eyes widened. "'Ere, who you calling an oaf? You'd better watch your tongue or I'll—"

"Constable," Cecily said hastily, "we have something to show you. Please come with us."

Northcott scowled at her. "I already told you, Mrs. Sinclair—"

"It's another body, you fool," Baxter muttered fiercely. "For God's sake, man, shut up for once and do your job."

Northcott drew himself up, throwing his shoulders back with a belligerent stance. "Well, I can see that the Smoke hasn't done much for your manners, Mr. Baxter. May I remind you that you are h'addressing an officer of the law. I could run you in for that remark, I could. I—"

He broke off and turned to look at Cecily. After a long pause, he whispered, "Another body?"

Cecily nodded. "At least, we think it is."

"Where?" Northcott demanded hoarsely.

"In the graveyard," Phoebe piped up.

Northcott scowled. "Is this some sort of prank? If so, I—"

"It's not a prank, Constable." Cecily glanced over to where the girls were still arguing. "If you'll come with us, we'll show you where it is."

For a moment it looked as if the constable would argue, but with another loud sigh he set off for the graveyard. Cecily and the others silently trooped behind.

Pausing at the edge of the graves, the constable glared at Cecily. "All right, and which dead body am I supposed to look at, then? Seeing as how there are so many, like."

"Over here, Constable." Leading the way, she paused at the site of the fresh grave. "The vicar assures me that this one is not supposed to be here," she announced.

Northcott looked puzzled. "Not supposed to be here?"

"It wasn't here yesterday," Cecily said.

"And we haven't had a funeral in six weeks," Algie added helpfully.

Northcott stared at the grave for several long seconds. "Have you got a couple of shovels we can use, Vicar?"

Algie turned green, but nodded valiantly. "I'll bring them, but please don't ask me to . . . ah . . . help dig this up. As a man of God I—"

"Don't worry," the constable muttered. "Mr. Baxter has a good pair of shoulders on him. He can help me."

Cecily looked anxiously at Baxter, who looked as if he might refuse. Catching Cecily's eye, however, he said reluctantly, "Oh, very well."

"Well, I'm going back with Algie," Phoebe said, beginning to look as ill as her son. "I really don't want to watch you dig up whatever is in there."

"I'll come and tell you when it's over," Cecily offered.

"I think it might be best if you wait with Mrs. Carter-Holmes," Baxter said quietly.

"No doubt you do," Cecily gave him a determined smile. "Wild horses, however, would not keep me away from this."

"I'll fetch the shovels," Baxter said grimly and followed Algie and Phoebe back to the vicarage. He returned shortly, and, after handing a shovel to Northcott, proceeded to dig.

Cecily said nothing as the two men labored over the grave. The earth was still wet from the night's rain, and clods of mud hit the ground with a resounding thud. After several anxious minutes had passed, Baxter uttered a short exclamation.

Peering over his shoulder, Cecily could just see the outline of a limp, white hand lying on top of the dark, damp earth. Then the constable leaned over and cleaned away the dirt from the frozen face.

Moving closer, Cecily held her breath and looked down at the mud-streaked, ashen features. "Oh, my Lord," she whispered. "It's Sid Barker."

CHAPTER

❈ 16 ❈

"You know this chap?" P.C. Northcott asked as Cecily straightened.

She drew in a long, slow breath of refreshing air. "Yes," she said quietly. "He's a guest at my hotel, I'm afraid."

"Not anymore, he's not." The constable threw down his shovel. "I wonder if Prestwick is still here," he muttered. "I'd better go and look for him." He gave Baxter a stern look. "Can I trust you to stand guard over this here body until I get back?"

"Indisputably," Baxter replied stiffly.

Northcott looked as if he wasn't sure what the word meant. After a short pause, however, he must have decided it was safe to leave. Without another word he lumbered off across the grass at a fair speed, considering his weight.

Baxter muttered something under his breath. Judging by his tone, Cecily thought, perhaps it was just as well she hadn't heard.

"You are not feeling faint, are you, Cecily?" he said as she moved away from the makeshift grave. "You look a trifle pale."

"No, I won't faint." She smiled at him. "After all, it's not the first dead body I've seen."

"I'm surprised you're not scrabbling about in his pockets before the constable gets back with Dr. Adonis."

She arched an eyebrow at him. "My, my, Baxter, you are having a bad day. First the constable, now the good doctor. How tiresome to have to deal with two archenemies at once."

Baxter stretched his neck above his collar. He hadn't looked that discomfited with her since he'd arrived in Badgers End. "I heartily dislike both men, yes," he said stiffly. "I have my reasons, however."

"I am aware of your reasons for detesting the constable," Cecily said, knowing she was pursuing a painful subject for him. Nevertheless, for some strange reason she felt compelled to press on. "After all, Stanley Northcott stole your only true love away from you. It's understandable you should hold a great deal of bitterness against him. The doctor, on the other hand, has not wronged you, to my knowledge."

Seeing the dangerous light in Baxter's eyes, she wished heartily now that she'd let the matter alone. "I do believe I am entitled to my opinion," he said, his voice tight. "Since you have brought up the subject, however, I will enlighten you. I dislike the doctor because I have a feeling that history might repeat itself."

She stared at him, once more rendered speechless by his innuendo. Could he be saying what she fervently hoped he was saying? Just once, she thought in frustration, she would dearly like to hear him say exactly what he meant, instead of hiding behind a host of insinuations. He was driving her quite insane.

She was about to tell him so when she caught sight of the constable hurrying across the grass toward them, with the doctor following close behind.

Upon reaching her, Dr. Prestwick greeted her with a fond smile. "My dear Cecily, I was beginning to think I would have to leave without seeing you," he said as she offered him her hand. Bending from the waist, he pressed his mouth to her fingers.

"I noticed you were rather occupied," Cecily said, aware of Baxter's scorching glare. "I trust you enjoyed the ceremony?"

"Most delightful. I can't remember when I've had such fun. Those remarkable lady bicyclists are most interesting, very entertaining indeed."

P.C. Northcott loudly cleared his throat. "If you wouldn't mind, sir, the body is over here."

"Oh, yes, quite." Prestwick dropped Cecily's hand with a rueful sigh. "I regret that you had to be present at such a gruesome find, my dear. Perhaps you and Mr. Baxter should leave now, rather than be caused any more unpleasantness."

Cecily exchanged a glance with Baxter, then lifted her chin. "I would prefer to wait, Kevin. Since Mr. Barker was a guest at my hotel, I feel obligated to know exactly how he died."

Prestwick looked wary. "I might not be able to divulge that information," he said quietly, sending a sideways glance at Northcott.

"I'm sure the constable will not mind if we stay. After all, there is no need to mention to the inspector that we were present. I'm sure there are many times when something is inadvertently omitted from a report."

She waited, while Northcott fidgeted on his feet. She could tell he knew quite well that she referred to his habit of dropping into the kitchen for a cup of tea and a piece of Mrs. Chubb's Dundee cake when he was supposed to be on duty.

"I don't reckon it'll do any harm," he mumbled at last. "Just as long as you refrain from mentioning it to anyone else."

"Of course, Constable," Cecily said, well pleased with herself. "I wouldn't dream of it. After all, it's no one's business but ours, is it, Baxter?"

"No, madam," Baxter muttered.

It was the first time he'd addressed her as such since he'd left her employ. His sarcasm wasn't lost on her, but she chose to ignore it.

She watched as Prestwick knelt at the graveside and began to examine the body. After what seemed a very long time, while everyone stood silent, the doctor got back to his feet and brushed the dirt from his trousers.

"I won't know for certain until I make a more thorough examination," he said, addressing the constable. "It would seem, however, that the cause of death was a severe blow to the back of the head."

"Hmmm." The constable stroked his bushy beard with stubby fingers. "Same way Will Jones died. Odd, that, wouldn't you say?"

"Very odd. Too much to be a coincidence, I would say."

The constable looked startled. Apparently forgetting about Cecily and Baxter, he said hoarsely, "You think it was the same bloke what done both murders?"

Prestwick shrugged and sent a warning glance in Cecily's direction. "All I can say is that it seems to be the same method."

Northcott appeared to collect himself. "Yes, well, thank you, Doctor. Perhaps you'll give me a hand with this here body? I need to get him down to the station and all I has is me bicycle. I don't want to leave a dead body around for everyone to gawk at."

"Not at all, Constable. Perhaps we can ask the vicar to borrow a sheet?"

"Right. I'll take care of that right away." Northcott touched the peak of his helmet. "Good day, Mrs. Sinclair, Mr. Baxter."

Taking the hint, Cecily said good-bye to the doctor, trying not to notice that Baxter gave him no more than a curt nod. She was anxious now to return to the hotel. She had something of importance to discuss with Baxter, and it simply couldn't wait.

"Thanks for going to the church with me, Ned," Gertie said as she walked with him across the yard to the kitchen door. "I had a bloody good time, I did. Thank goodness Ethel didn't mind looking after the twins. Been a bleeding long time since I was out enjoying meself."

"Been my pleasure, me darlin'," Ned said cheerfully. "Had a good old chuckle, didn't we?"

"Yeah." Gertie smiled at the memory. "'Specially the bleeding dancing. I haven't danced like that in me blinking life before."

"You were smashing, luv. Real light on the old plates, you are."

"So are you." She grinned at him. "You never told me you could dance."

"You never asked." He winked at her. "You should see me in the ballroom. Proper fancy, I am. We'll have to take a whirl around the floor sometime."

"Yeah, that'd be really nice." She laughed. "Some of

them looked bleeding dopey trying to do that dance. Did you see the constable? His flipping helmet kept slipping off his head. He looked bleeding stupid if you ask me."

To her surprise, Ned's expression changed at once. "All bloody bobbies are stupid. I hate the lot of 'em."

Gertie felt a small quiver of alarm. She'd almost forgotten her initial mistrust of Ned Harris. The sight of that scowl on his face, however, brought the feeling back again. "Why?" she asked bluntly. "What've they ever done to you?"

"They tried to nab me for something I didn't do, that's what."

Shocked, Gertie stopped short. "They bloody what?"

Ned hunched his shoulders and thrust his hands into the pockets of his trousers. "They said I nicked a gentleman's watch."

Gertie gasped. "You didn't, did you?"

Ned gave her a disgusted look. "'Course I didn't. I saw the bugger snatch it. It was in the middle of Piccadilly Circus. He punched the toff in the back, then reached around and tore his watch off the chain. He was off with it before the poor bloke knew what was happening."

"Go on," Gertie said breathlessly. "What happened then?"

"Well, I took off after him, didn't I? Caught up with him, too. I was struggling with him, like, trying to get the watch back, when the bastard just gave it to me and scarpered. That was when I saw the bobby coming."

"And he said you took it?"

"Yeah. Put me in prison for six months."

"But didn't you bleeding tell him it weren't you?"

"I reckon he knew it wasn't me. He just wanted to look good to his mates, that was all."

"Well, what about the bloody toff? Didn't he say it weren't you?"

Ned shrugged. "He said he didn't see who it was.

Anyhow, the magistrate said as how I looked guilty and that I didn't look like the sort what would be Sir Galahad, so he sent me to prison."

"That's bloody awful," Gertie said, outraged by the blatant injustice. "That bleeding bobby should be locked up and that blinking judge."

She started when Ned suddenly turned to her and grasped her by the shoulders. "You're not to tell no one," he said fiercely. No one, you hear me?"

"'Ere," Gertie said, struggling to free herself from his painful grip, "you're bloody hurting me. Get your flipping hands off me, Ned Harris."

"Sorry." Ned dropped his hands at once. "It was why I left London, see, and came down here. I couldn't get a job in the Smoke no more after that. No one would believe I didn't do it. I don't want to lose this job here now. I like working at the Pennyfoot."

Gertie rubbed her sore shoulder. "I won't bleeding tell no one, silly. I swear. Does madam know about it?"

"No, and I don't want her to know. I don't want no one to know." He gave her a look that made her belly warm. "I don't really know why I told you. It's just that I sort of feel comfortable when I'm with you."

She smiled at him. "I feel comfortable with you, too, Ned Harris. And I do bloody believe you didn't do it, so there."

He didn't smile. He just went on looking at her with a daft look in his eyes that made her feel all funny inside. "Somehow," he said softly, "I knew you would."

Arriving back at the hotel, Cecily invited Baxter to join her for afternoon tea again. "In the conservatory," she added primly, just to make things clear.

Baxter merely nodded. He seemed preoccupied, as if mulling something over in his mind. Wondering if he was displeased with her in some way, Cecily uneasily led him to the conservatory.

Hidden in the corner behind a huge aspidistra, she felt secure enough in their privacy to question him about it. "Have I said something to upset you, Baxter?" she inquired after Doris had left them alone with a table laden with delicacies. "If so, I should be obliged if you would enlighten me."

He looked at her, his face softening into a smile. "No, Cecily, you have not. I have simply been wrestling with a certain issue that I hope will be resolved very soon. Perhaps this very afternoon, in fact, if I might have your attention for a while?"

Her heart skipped a beat. Was he about to make his feelings clear? If so, she really didn't know what she would say. She wasn't prepared for such a momentous occasion. She needed more notice, so as to compose herself and behave calmly and rationally.

He had said that he would discuss matters with her on Saturday. This was only Friday. She simply wasn't prepared. "Of course," she blurted out, "but first I have something I want to discuss with you."

The light in his eyes faded, and she felt a sharp stab of regret. "By all means," he murmured. "The matter can wait."

"On the other hand," she said lamely, "if the matter is of importance . . ."

Baxter shook his head. "It can wait," he said firmly. "What was it you wanted to discuss with me?"

She let out a small sigh. Sometimes she found it difficult to understand herself. Leaning forward, she whispered, "I think I know who killed Sid Barker. Very likely Will Jones, as well."

Baxter's eyebrows rose. "When did you discover this?"

"At the church." Cecily reached for the milk jug and poured a little in each teacup. "I saw footprints around the grave site."

"I imagine there were several footprints around the grave site," Baxter said, watching her pour the tea from the silver teapot.

"Of course there were." Cecily sat the teapot down and handed him the cup and saucer. There were, however, only one set of footprints with high heels."

Baxter looked startled. "High heels?"

Cecily offered him the plate of sandwiches. "I saw several prints of a flat sole, together with a much deeper indent of a heel. The earth was soft because of the rain. I didn't see any marks of a body being dragged to the grave, so I assume it was carried there. The extra weight made the heels sink into the earth. They were quite definitely high heels."

Baxter took a couple of the sandwiches and laid them on his plate. "Are you saying that a woman killed Sid Barker, carried him to the graveyard, dug a grave, and buried him there?"

"That's exactly what I'm saying. Sid Barker was not a heavy man. In fact, he looked rather fragile. It wouldn't have been that difficult for a fairly strong woman to carry him there."

"What about Mrs. Carter-Holmes? Could they be her footprints? She was tramping around the grave, as well."

Cecily shook her head. "Phoebe always wears flat heels. She prefers to look petite." She stared at the sandwiches for a moment, then chose a sardine and tomato. "I think the footprints belonged to Primrose Parsons."

Baxter swallowed the last bite of his sandwich. "Miss Parsons? Well, she's certainly husky enough to have carried a dead body across a wet graveyard. But why would she want to kill Sid Barker?"

"I'm not certain about that," Cecily admitted. "But I do know they detested each other. I heard them arguing once, remember? They were quite insulting to each other. Then there's the fact that Primrose Parsons was absent from the dining room the night of the feast."

"But Sid Barker wasn't killed until yesterday, presumably."

Cecily sighed. "Yes, I know. I saw Sid myself yesterday morning. The point is, suppose that Miss Parsons is the one who stole the cup. At first I thought Sid Barker had stolen it, but now I think it was Miss Parsons who stole it and killed Will Jones when he discovered her taking it. Perhaps Sid Barker found out about it, and she had to kill him, too."

"Our Miss Parsons has been a very busy lady," Baxter said, reaching for his teacup. "This is all conjecture, however. How do you propose to prove what you suspect?"

"We'll have to search her room, of course. If I'm right, we should find a pair of high-heeled shoes covered in mud, as well as the stolen chalice." Cecily beamed at him. "Come now, Baxter, take that frown off your face. Didn't you say yourself that you missed our little adventures? Well, here's your chance to enjoy one more."

Very slowly, Baxter put down his cup. "I suppose there is no point in objecting to this escapade. If I don't agree to help, you will simply go ahead and search the room all by yourself, I presume?"

"All by myself," Cecily said smugly.

After a long, thoughtful pause, he nodded. "Very well. It was inevitable, I suppose. A fitting ending, no doubt."

Cecily's smile vanished. Now what did he mean by those cryptic words? Was he telling her he was never coming back to Badgers End? Could she have been quite wrong about his intentions after all?

Perhaps his affectionate attitude had been nothing more than a product of city sophistication. In two days he would return to his new life. Perhaps this was his way of saying good-bye.

If so, she now knew she would be devastated. Now that she was finally sure of her feelings for him, it seemed that she might lose him after all.

CHAPTER

✠ 17 ✠

Cecily waited until everyone was in the dining room before embarking upon her quest. Baxter hovered in the hallway for a while, in order to make certain that Miss Parsons joined her companions and was not taking the meal in her room. Assured of that, he joined Cecily, and the two of them then quickly mounted the stairs.

"This is just like old times, Baxter," Cecily whispered as they made their way down the hallway to Primrose Parsons's room. "Thank goodness Miss Parsons has a room to herself. Everyone else, with the exception of the bishop, is either with their husband or sharing with a friend."

"I can't imagine Miss Parsons with a husband," Baxter muttered, glancing back over his shoulder. "To be quite frank, that woman scares me to death. Just envision waking up in the morning to find that face lying next to you."

Shocked by the comment, Cecily looked up at him. "I had no idea you envisioned any such thing, Baxter."

He raised an eyebrow. "No doubt you would be astounded if you knew what I envisioned."

Discomfited, she dropped her gaze. "No doubt I would," she murmured. She had been quite wrong. This wasn't like old times at all. Somehow this particular escapade had taken on an anticipation such as she'd never experienced before. Which was odd, considering how many times she and Baxter had been obliged to search a guest's room for evidence.

Fitting the master key into the lock of Miss Parsons's door, Cecily turned it and then entered. Baxter followed close behind, and for once seemed to have no compunction about being in a closed room with her. Before, the thought of such a thing had caused him concern. Apparently his new life had greatly relaxed his sense of propriety. The thought made Cecily extremely nervous.

She kept her distance as she gazed around. "Perhaps you should search under the bed," she told him, "while I search the wardrobe. Those are the two most likely places to find the shoes."

Baxter obediently lowered himself to his hands and knees and peered under the bed. "There are two pairs of shoes here," he announced and reached under the bed for them.

Cecily moved closer to take a look at them. They were serviceable walking shoes with high-buttoned tops. "Both have flat heels," she said with a sigh. "Perhaps I shall find something in the wardrobe. We must take care to put the shoes back in exactly the same position."

She left him to replace the shoes and opened the wardrobe. Three more pairs of shoes sat on the upper shelf—two pairs of evening shoes and a pair of fashionable dress shoes.

Disappointed, Cecily closed the wardrobe. "All of the shoes have flat heels," she said as Baxter got to his feet and dusted down his trousers with the flat of his palms.

"Perhaps she hid the ones she wore," he suggested, sending a wary glance at the door. "Or perhaps she is wearing them tonight."

Cecily shook her head. "I saw her come down the stairs. She is wearing flat-heeled shoes tonight, also. Since she is an unusually tall woman, it's logical to suppose she would shun high heels altogether."

"You are reasonably tall," Baxter pointed out, "yet you wear them."

She gave him a startled look. "I'm surprised you noticed."

"As I've told you many times, I notice many things."

"Well, in any case, I'm not as tall as Miss Parsons. I think we have to accept the fact that she did not make those footprints around the grave."

"Then we can leave?" Baxter asked hopefully. "I have an uneasy feeling that the lady might very well come back and find us lurking around in her bedroom."

"That would indeed put us both in rather a compromising position," Cecily said with a trace of irony.

"It would not be the first time."

Something in his expression arrested her. "No," she said softly, "it would not."

The silence in the room seemed to go on for a very long time. She could not seem to tear her gaze from his face, though she detected a look of purpose in his eyes that set her heart pounding much too fast.

The muffled sound of laughter from somewhere outside

broke the trance. "We had best leave at once," Baxter whispered urgently.

Still greatly unsettled, she nodded and moved stealthily over to the door. Putting her ear close to the panel, she listened. The voices seemed to be at a distance. "I'll leave," she said quietly, "then, after a moment or two, you can follow."

"Very well. Please, Cecily, do be careful."

She smiled at that. "Am I not always careful?" She opened the door and slipped outside without waiting for his answer.

On the other side of the staircase, three women stood laughing and chattering together. It was doubtful that they could see her clearly in the dim shadows cast by the gas lamps. Nevertheless, Cecily quickly moved toward the stairs.

The women turned to look at her as she approached them, and she positioned herself so that their attention was directed away from the hallway. "I hope you enjoyed your meal, ladies," she inquired brightly. "Michel went to great pains to find fresh salmon for tonight's dinner."

There were cries of appreciation from the three ladies. Over their shoulders Cecily saw Baxter sneak from the room and move silently toward the staircase.

"I have just been up to the roof garden," Cecily said, smiling at the ladies. "Have any of you visited it yet? It really is quite unique. A little haven between the roofs, with a wonderful display of roses planted in half barrels. The view is quite spectacular."

Baxter rolled his eyes to the ceiling, then swiftly and without a sound he descended the stairs.

Cecily pointed out the curtain that hid the steps to the roof garden and left the twittering ladies to explore on their own. She found Baxter waiting for her at the foot of the stairs.

"Shall we retire to the library?" she said as guests streamed past them on their way from the dining room. "I can have Mrs. Chubb send up a tray if you are hungry. Or would you prefer to eat at the George and Dragon?"

Baxter pulled a face. "The food at the pub has deteriorated since your son left. I much prefer Michel's cooking." He walked with her down the hallway to the library. "You haven't mentioned Master Michael since I arrived. I trust your son is doing well?"

"Very well, from what I hear." Cecily paused long enough to order a tray from Daisy—or Doris—she wasn't quite sure which. There were times when she could tell her twin housemaids apart, usually when they were together. When they were separated, she found it difficult sometimes to know if she was addressing Doris or Daisy.

Entering the library a few minutes later, she sat down at her usual spot at the end of the long table. Baxter took a seat at her right hand. She still found it strange to see him seated there. For years he had refused to sit in her presence, unless they were dining together or riding in the trap, of course.

"Simani is expecting the baby any time now," she said quietly. "My only regret is that I shall not see my first grandchild born. I suppose it is fitting that he be born in Africa. It is, after all, the place of his mother's birth."

She was unsettled again when Baxter laid his hand over hers and gave it a gentle squeeze. "I know how the absence of your sons pains you. I know what it is to be without a family."

Cecily gave him a rueful smile. "Our staff here at the Pennyfoot are our family, Baxter. We have always regarded them as such."

"Not for much longer." He removed his hand from hers. "Now, what do you propose to do about your theory regarding the murder of Will Jones?"

She took her time in answering him. His remark about no longer regarding the staff of the Pennyfoot as his family affected her deeply. It seemed one more indication that on Sunday Baxter intended to return to the city, severing his ties with Badgers End and the Pennyfoot completely.

Finally, as he continued to look at her expectantly, she answered him. "Since Sid Barker appears to be a victim and therefore not the murderer, and we have more or less concluded that Miss Parsons is not the culprit, that leaves only Malcolm Ridlington on my list of possible suspects. I am quite sure that Malcolm does not wear high heels."

"Are you that certain the murderer wore high heels?"

Cecily nodded. "If there is one thing I have learned in my efforts to solve a murder, it is to look for something that is out of place. Those footprints were put there after the rain on Thursday night. The only people to go near the grave after that were Phoebe, Algie, and ourselves—none of whom were wearing high heels."

She transferred her gaze to the portrait of her late husband that hung over the marble fireplace. "I'm very much afraid," she said quietly, "that for once I must admit defeat."

Cecily awoke the next morning with a sense of impending doom. At first she thought it was the knowledge that she would have to go to Phoebe and tell her that she had been unable to unearth the chalice. Algie would have to inform the bishop that his precious relic had been stolen.

The constable would also have to be informed. P.C. Northcott was not going to be happy to know she had kept the news from him for several days. Worse, Inspector Cranshaw would no doubt be breathing down her neck, chastising her for once more interfering in police business.

It wasn't the lecture she minded so much, Cecily thought as she washed and dressed in her favorite blue dotted-swiss frock, it was the veiled threat behind the words. Inspector Cranshaw never missed an opportunity to remind her that should he choose to do so, he could quite easily find good reason to close down the Pennyfoot Hotel.

Were it not for the fact that the Pennyfoot's customers were largely members of the aristocracy, the nefarious goings-on within the hotel's walls would be considered highly suspect. Cecily was well aware that the Pennyfoot's security hung by a thin thread. Nevertheless, it was because of her tolerance of such delicate situations that the wealthy patronized the hotel. A simple matter of supply and demand.

Studying her image in the mirror, however, she knew that it was none of these problems that troubled her this morning. Today was Saturday, when Baxter had promised to have an important discussion with her.

When he had left her employ more than three months ago, he had been quite secretive about his plans. It had been so unlike him that Cecily had half expected him to return that very day to explain his odd behavior. Instead, he had waited three months before returning.

She had the dismal feeling that he intended to give her a formal farewell. Apparently his new life in London had changed his entire personality. He was no longer the Baxter she once knew and still loved. He was a different man with a broader outlook on life and perhaps new horizons.

He might well have a lady friend in the city. The thought almost paralyzed her with misery. Yet, if that were so, how could he explain that odd remark in the graveyard yesterday about history repeating itself? Unless he was generalizing about philandering men.

Cecily turned away from the mirror with a muttered "Piffle!" This was not the time to fret over what might or might not be. She had to get over to the church and confess her failure to Phoebe and Algie. After that she would worry about what Baxter had to say to her.

By the time she arrived at the church, she was feeling a little better. The balmy air of the late summer morning cleared her mind, and she was able to think rationally once more. Whatever Baxter's decision, she had to accept it.

She still had the Pennyfoot, and the hotel was her life's blood. As long as she could continue to live and work with her substitute family, she could be happy. If she ever had to do without them, she thought as she marched briskly up the gravel path to the vicarage, that would certainly be a death blow.

Phoebe answered the door to her knock, her face lighting up with hope. "You found it?" she exclaimed as she stepped back to allow Cecily to enter the tiny living room.

"I'm afraid not." Watching her friend's face fall, Cecily felt a deep sense of frustration. Of all times to fail, letting down a friend had to be the very worst. "I"m so very sorry," she said as Phoebe sank into an armchair. "I thought I had the solution until last night. Now there just isn't any more time."

Phoebe looked up, her eyes suspiciously bright. "It's quite all right, Cecily. I know you did your very best. I only hope Algie is exaggerating when he says we might lose the vicarage. After all, as I have already said, I can't see how they can blame us when the bishop locked up the case himself."

"I feel certain Algie is worrying unnecessarily," Cecily said firmly.

"Maybe so. What worries me is that Algie thinks he might actually be blamed for stealing the cup himself."

"I hardly think that will happen." Cecily sat herself next to Phoebe. "When is the bishop due to arrive?"

"Within the next half hour." She glanced at the window.

"In fact, I should be getting over to the church. Algie is there now, waiting for him." She looked mournfully at Cecily. "Algie is not feeling very well this morning. He hasn't uttered a word since he came downstairs."

"I'm so sorry." Cecily wished she didn't feel so guilty. "Would you like me to wait for the bishop with you? Perhaps if I'm there as well, Algie won't feel quite so insecure."

"Thank you, Cecily. That would be very nice." Phoebe looked tired as she got to her feet. "I'm not at all sure I can handle Algie when he gets like this. I'd appreciate your help."

Walking along the path to the church, Cecily told Phoebe about her theory of the footprints.

"I suppose it must have been Mrs. Puckett's shoes," Phoebe said as they reached the porch. "She was at the grave next to the new one the day before we found it. I believe I told you."

"Yes, you did," Cecily said, feeling frustrated. There had to be an answer somewhere. She was simply missing something, that was all.

They entered the porch together, and Phoebe stood back to allow Cecily to move ahead into the church.

Algie was seated in the front pew, his head buried in his hands. He lifted his head sharply as Cecily walked down the aisle, her heels clicking loudly in the silence of the church. Phoebe followed more quietly behind.

"Good morning, Vicar," Cecily said as he rose to his feet.

He nodded. "G-g-good m-m-m . . ." He stopped, his mouth opening and shutting, his glasses trembling on the end of his nose.

"Deep breaths, Algie," Phoebe said crossly. "You'll never get anything out if you don't take deep breaths."

Algie shut his mouth tight and gave his mother a look that

suggested if he had his way, he'd never utter another sound.

"I'm sorry, Algie," Cecily said gently. "I did my best to find the chalice, but I'm afraid it was impossible. Can I look at the fake one while we're waiting for the bishop?"

Algie nodded and waved his hand in the direction of the pedestal.

Moving over to it, Cecily peered at the cup. It looked much the same, except that on closer inspection the jewels seemed dull and lifeless, and the gold just a little too bright to be real.

"There's the dent in the side," Phoebe said, reaching up to shift the case around. "We've had it pointed toward the back so that no one would notice it."

Cecily looked at the dent. It was quite obvious that the cup was made of some kind of fragile material. Algie was probably right. The fake chalice was most likely made of cheap tin.

Phoebe shifted the case back so that the dent was hidden from view. "I really don't know if Algie will be able to explain things to the bishop," she said, looking worried. "He insists on telling the man himself, but when he gets extremely nervous like this he finds it almost impossible to speak legibly."

"I think we must let him try," Cecily said, looking over at the distressed vicar, who had sunk down on the pew again. "All we can do is stand by and be ready to offer him comfort once the ordeal is over."

Phoebe reluctantly nodded. "I'm afraid you are right. I do feel awful for him, though. He has absolutely dreaded this moment for days. I don't think he has slept at all. If it weren't for those dreadful girls, he would never have known the chalice was a fake, and I can't help wondering if that would have been better. At the very least he would have had a good night's sleep. Just look at him. He's a perfect wreck."

"I'm sure he'll be all right once he faces the bishop," Cecily said, not sure of that at all. "Somehow Algie always manages to rise to the occasion. No matter how nervous he gets."

The door of the porch slammed just then, forcing Algie to utter a frightened squeak. Then the voice of doom spoke from the doorway.

"Is anyone there?" the bishop called out. "I've arrived to collect the chalice."

CHAPTER

❈ 18 ❈

For several seconds no one said anything, then Phoebe called out tremulously, "Here we are, Bishop! We have been waiting for you."

Algie struggled to his feet and gave his mother a look that clearly told her to let him handle matters. Phoebe shut her mouth in a tight little line as the bishop hurried down the aisle toward them, his footsteps ringing out like a dire warning.

Algie stepped out into the middle of the aisle and faced the advancing man, looking as if he were confronting a runaway steam train.

The bishop stopped abruptly when it became clear that Algie was not about to move. "Good morning, Vicar," he said uncertainly.

Algie opened his mouth. "B-b-b-ish-sh. . . ."

The bishop sighed. "All right, Vicar, slow down. Take one word at a time."

Algie nodded, while Phoebe made a little moaning sound. Distracted, Algie turned his head to look at her. Phoebe started to say something, but Algie stopped her with a frantic shake of his head. Turning back to the bishop, he tried again. Once more, all that he could manage was a rasping stutter.

"My good man," the bishop said, reaching out to pat him on the shoulder, "I appreciate the effort. Let us just take it as said, shall we? It has been a pleasure for me also. But now I must leave."

"B-b-b-b-ut—" Algie began again, only to be rather abruptly brushed aside by the bishop. "I am sorry, Vicar, but I really can't delay any longer. I plan to catch the evening train and I still have to pack all my belongings."

"Bishop," Phoebe said, catching his sleeve, "I really think you should hear what Algie has to say. It is quite important."

Again the bishop halted, his frown quite formidable. "Then perhaps, Mrs. Carter-Holmes," he said carefully, "you would be good enough to tell me yourself what it is the vicar is trying to say."

Algie squeaked and violently shook his head. Yet again he tried valiantly to get out the words, and Cecily wished desperately she could do something to help. It was agonizing to stand there and watch the poor man struggle. Poor Phoebe had to be beside herself with anxiety.

With a muttered exclamation of impatience, the bishop turned and hurried over to the pedestal. In silence, Cecily watched with Phoebe and a trembling Algie as the bishop took a key from his pocket and unlocked the lengthy chain. Carefully he wound the chain around the case, then grasped it with both arms and lifted it free of the pedestal.

"Now," he said briskly as he marched toward them, "I do want to thank you, Vicar, for taking care of the chalice. I have enjoyed my brief stay in Badgers End and look forward to returning some day."

He glanced over at Cecily. "I shall no doubt see you again before I leave the hotel, Mrs. Sinclair?"

"I'm sure you will, Bishop," Cecily murmured.

"Good day, then, Mrs. Carter-Holmes, Vicar. It has been a pleasure." With that, he strode off up the aisle.

Algie let out a whimper and stumbled after him, still trying to get a comprehensible word out of his uncooperative mouth.

"Oh, dear," Phoebe muttered, one hand clutching her lace-bound throat. "I shall have to tell the bishop myself, after all."

Cecily laid a hand on her arm. "Not quite yet, Phoebe," she said quietly. "In fact, I think you had better stop Algie from trying to say anything more. He is liable to choke himself if he continues to struggle on like that."

"But, Cecily," Phoebe said, darting a frantic look at the departing bishop, "what will happen when the bishop discovers the chalice is a fake? He will be even angrier that we didn't tell him at once. Algie is quite certain he will be accused of stealing the cup himself."

"Well, Algie can rest assured on that count." Cecily gave Phoebe's arm a little shake. "Please, Phoebe, try to quiet Algie. I am quite worried about him."

With a helpless shake of her head, Phoebe hurried after her son. She caught up with him by the door and led him back down the aisle. He was ashen-faced and looked close to tears.

Cecily gave him a sympathetic smile. "Try not to worry, Vicar," she said as he stared at her with the anxious eyes of a small boy. "We still have time before the bishop's train leaves, and I think I just might be able to find the chalice before then."

Phoebe uttered an exclamation of surprise. "Do you really think you can, Cecily? I thought you said it was impossible."

"There is one thing I should take care to remember," Cecily said, tugging her gloves closer to her elbows. "There are very few things, indeed, that are impossible. I tend to forget that at times."

Leaving Phoebe and Algie staring after her, she quickly left the church. She had no time to waste if she were to solve this puzzle and return the chalice to its rightful owner.

"What, you here again?" Mrs. Chubb said good-naturedly when she spotted Ethel in the kitchen. "You spend more time here lately than you do at home. What does Joe say to that?"

Ethel shrugged. "He don't mind," she said airily. "We have the housekeeper to take care of the house, and he's always busy with the farm. He's getting ready to harvest right now, so I won't see him from dawn to dusk anyhow. Always something with a farm, it is. I never knew it was so much hard work."

"It is that." Mrs. Chubb studied the list of supplies in her hand. "We need some more marmalade," she muttered. "And chutney. I knew there was something else."

A wail came from the corner where Daisy was trying to keep the twins happy with a few silver serviette rings strung on a string.

Gertie looked up from the pile of silverware she was sorting out. "Doesn't Joe want you to help him with the flipping work?"

Ethel shook her head. "He knows I'd rather work here. I never did like messing about outdoors."

"I wish you could bleeding work here," Gertie mumbled. "Things haven't been the bloody same since you left."

"I don't suppose madam would let me work for half pay?" Ethel said hopefully. "I get so bored at home by myself. I wouldn't need a lot, as long as Joe's doing all right with the farm."

Both twins wailed as Gertie dropped a pile of forks on the table with a clatter. "Wait a minute, I got a bloody idea," she said, her voice high with excitement.

Both Ethel and Mrs. Chubb looked at her.

"Well, go on, girl, tell us what it is," Mrs. Chubb said impatiently.

"Well, Daisy's always saying as how she wants to take care of the babies all the time, like a flipping nanny. What if Daisy works for me instead of madam? Ethel could have Daisy's job, and both me and Ethel could give some of our wages to Daisy. That way we could all bloody work here, and it wouldn't cost madam any more."

Daisy jumped to her feet, her face radiant. "I'd really, really like that, Miss Brown. I could manage with less pay, since Doris and I share the money anyway."

"And that way the babies wouldn't be underfoot in the kitchen all the time," Mrs. Chubb said, nodding her head. "I think madam might accept that. I'll have a word with her about it this very afternoon."

Ethel and Gertie grinned at each other. "We could have some bloody good times again," Gertie said, chuckling with glee.

"Just as long as you both get some work done," Mrs. Chubb warned sharply. "I don't want to be chasing after you all the time, like I did before."

"Nah," Gertie said, winking at Ethel. "We're a lot bleeding older and wiser now, ain't we, Ethel?"

"That's what concerns me," Mrs. Chubb muttered.

Gertie wasn't listening. Life was beginning to look awfully good again. If madam agreed to her idea, her problem with the babies would be solved, she and Ethel would be together again, and what's more, Ned Harris really liked her, she could tell. It would be just like old times. Only better.

Arriving back at the hotel, Cecily noted that she had at least an hour to wait until Baxter arrived for their discussion. In her present state of uncertainty about his intentions, she wasn't sure whether she was looking forward to the meeting or dreading it. Nevertheless, she was anxious to see him. She had one last favor to ask of him if, indeed, it would be the last she saw of him.

Deciding that the anticipation would make her insane if she dwelt on it, she decided to kill the time by paying Malcolm a visit. He had been in her employ for almost a week, and it was time she took stock of his work.

Reaching the office, she gave the door a short tap and opened it without waiting for his response. He was seated at his desk, as usual, though he seemed to be absorbed in a novel of some sort. He rose quickly when she entered, stuffing the book into the drawer of his desk.

He seemed discomforted by her presence and avoided her gaze as she greeted him. "I do hope I'm not interrupting anything?" she added dryly.

"Er—no, madam. I was taking a short break."

"I see." She glanced down at the ledger in front of him. "How are the accounts coming along? Do you have them balanced yet? What can we expect in the way of profit this month?"

Malcolm cleared his throat. "We will not have a profit this month, madam. In fact, there will be a considerable loss. The cost of supplies and wages far outweigh the receipts, I'm afraid."

"That can't be," Cecily said sharply. "Even when the hotel is no more than half full, we manage to cover our expenses. You must have made a mistake."

"I do not make mistakes, madam." Malcolm's hostile eyes peered at her over the top of his glasses. "And, if I might add, I bitterly resent the accusation."

"In that case," Cecily said, doing her best to curb her irritation, "perhaps you should show me where the discrepancies are, so that we can rectify them in future."

Malcolm looked as if he would refuse, but when Cecily reached for the ledger and turned it around to look at it, he made no attempt to stop her.

"I can assure you, madam," he said stiffly, "you will find no fault with my figures. I did warn you that allowing guests into the hotel at a lower rate was a mistake."

Cecily lifted her chin. "Since our regular guests prefer not to visit the hotel during Saint Bartholomew's Week, it would seem prudent to fill the hotel with lower-paying guests rather than have the hotel stand empty, would it not?"

Malcolm lifted his shoulders in an insolent shrug.

Ignoring him, Cecily peered intently at the untidy columns, her gaze running down the scrawled figures. Everything appeared to be within reason, she noted, her heart sinking. Surely they couldn't have taken that large a loss on the week? They should have made at least a small profit.

Casting her eye along the balances column, she noticed a figure that made her frown. She flipped the page back to look at the previous page, then let it fall back into place.

"Mr. Ridlington," she said quietly, "please look at these balance columns and tell me what you see."

He did so, albeit with a sigh of impatience. Muttering so

low she could scarcely hear him, he read out the balances across the page.

When he reached the balance of receipts, she held up her hand. "That is the balance of receipts?"

"Yes, madam, that is the balance of receipts," Malcolm said nastily.

"Then perhaps you can tell me where the receipts are for the first three weeks of the month? Since the total of costs are for the entire month, shouldn't the total of receipts be also?"

Malcolm's face turned crimson. Avoiding her gaze, he muttered, "I see I neglected to bring forward the balance of the receipts from last week. My apologies, madam. It won't happen again."

She wasn't sure if her reaction was due to her manager's outrageous incompetence or her anxiety over the outcome of forthcoming events that afternoon. She only knew that she had finally and irrevocably had enough of Malcolm Ridlington.

"You can rest assured I shall take very good care that it won't happen again," she said evenly. "As of this moment, Mr. Ridlington, you are no longer in my employ."

Malcolm's jaw dropped. He started to speak, but she forestalled him.

"Please do not ask me for references, or I shall be forced to warn prospective employers of your gross ineptitude. I would suggest that you find another form of occupation, since you are clearly unsuited to making a living as an accountant."

Malcolm shut his mouth. He stood stiffly at attention, looking as if he would like to tear down the hotel with his bare hands.

"I expect you to leave these premises before the end of the day," Cecily said, moving to the door. "If not, you will be charged the appropriate rate for occupying a room. I will have your severance pay waiting for you at the front desk. Pick it up on your way out."

She left the office, trembling from head to foot. She had been determined not to let the man know he intimidated her, but now that it was finally over she felt like weeping. Once more she was without a manager. And very soon, she would possibly be seeing Baxter for the last time.

For the very first time since she and James had bought the Pennyfoot from the family of an impoverished earl, she wondered if the effort was worth the struggle. Much as she loved the hotel and its staff, much as she enjoyed the life, there were times when the fight to maintain the business seemed overwhelming.

And never more so than these past three months without the man who had come to mean so very much to her. "Oh, Baxter," she whispered in the lonely shadows of the hallway. "How can I go on without you now?"

CHAPTER

❖ 19 ❖

Baxter arrived shortly before the appointed time, looking extremely dapper in a smart city lounge suit and his homburg at a rakish angle on his head.

Ned opened the door to him, greeting the other man with his usual cheerful, "Watcha, Mr. Baxter! Nice whistle, that."

Waiting at the foot of the stairs, Cecily closed her eyes briefly. She half expected Baxter to reprimand Ned, but he said nothing as he stepped into the lobby.

At first glance, as he removed his hat and hung it on the hallstand, Cecily thought Baxter looked poised and self-assured. When he caught sight of her, however, she saw a look of apprehension flit across his face before he collected himself again.

Watching him smooth back his hair with his hand, she

was unsettled by that brief sign of anxiety. Apparently he was concerned about their forthcoming discussion. No doubt he was wondering how best to break the bad news to her.

Well, she'd faced bad news before, she told herself, lifting her chin, and she would do so again. After all, she had a business to run, and she could not allow her personal problems to interfere with that.

"Cecily," Baxter exclaimed as he reached her, "I do hope you haven't been waiting long for me?"

"Oh, no." She managed to smile up at him with apparent unconcern. "As a matter of fact, I have just come from my manager's office. Or I should say, my ex-manager's office."

Baxter gave a rueful shake of his head. "It is no longer my office, Cecily. You must think of it as Ridlington's office now."

"You don't understand." She reached for his arm and drew him further down the hallway, out of reach of Ned's curious ears. "Malcolm Ridlington is no longer in my employ," she added, lowering her voice. "I just gave him the sack."

"Did you, indeed," Baxter said softly with an odd gleam in his eye. "I wondered how long you would put up with the man's insolence and incompetence."

He looked so smug that she felt quite irritated. "Oh, very well, Baxter. I admit it. You were right, of course. The man is an ignorant fool. Perhaps you should hire the next manager for me, since you appear to have such a keen aptitude for judging character."

Baxter's eyebrows raised. "I think perhaps you are the one who is liverish today. Are you not feeling well?"

Cecily shrugged. "Merely tired, that's all."

"Ah." He studied her for a long moment. "Perhaps you would feel better if you smoked a cigar."

"A cigar will not help, I'm afraid."

"Then perhaps a visit to your favorite spot in the roof garden?" He cleared his throat, stretching his neck above his crisp white wing collar. "I would like to go up there again. I have many fond memories of the delightful conversations we have enjoyed there."

Was he planning to say good-bye, as she had feared all along? Determined to put a brave face on it, she gave a brisk nod. "I would like that. First of all, however, there is a small matter I must take care of, and I was wondering if I could count on your help . . . one last time."

If he noted the sarcasm in her voice, he gave no sign. "Whatever you wish, Cecily."

She wished for once that he'd refer to her as madam, as he used to do. The memory brought a swift twinge of regret, and she looked away, to where Ned still hovered in the doorway, trying to pretend he didn't see them standing there.

"I need to search another room," she said, her voice low enough to keep Ned from hearing her.

There was a long pause, and she wondered if he would refuse this time. "I was under the impression that you'd given up that particular quest," he said at last.

"I had." She looked back at him. "I have discovered some new evidence, however, that now makes me certain of the identity of the thief, if not the murderer."

"I see." He rocked back on his heels, his hands behind his back, in a gesture she had seen so often. "But you are still without the proof, I take it."

"Yes." She lifted her chin. "I am quite certain, however, that we shall find the proof in the room I intend to search."

"You are quite certain," Baxter repeated, sounding extremely skeptical.

"Absolutely certain. In fact, I have already sent for P.C.

Northcott. I would like to search the room now, so that I have the evidence to present to him when he arrives."

His expression changed to one of alarm. "You've sent for the constable? Isn't that taking an unnecessary risk? If you are mistaken—"

"I am not mistaken," Cecily said firmly. "In any case, I have no choice. Time is running out, and I cannot afford to wait another day."

To her relief, she saw that he was now taking her seriously. "I had hoped that yesterday would be the last time I ever had to indulge in such precarious business," he said, sending an anxious glance toward Ned. "Tell me, whose room are we to search?"

Cecily also glanced at the door, but Ned was now talking to the colonel, who had just entered the lobby. "Let us go upstairs," she said hurriedly. "I will tell you on the way."

Baxter was about to reply when Mrs. Chubb appeared at the top of the kitchen steps. "Oh, there you are, mum," she called out as she hurried toward them. "Might I have a quick word with you, if you please?"

Cecily uttered a sharp sigh. "Very well, Mrs. Chubb. If it won't take too long?"

"No, mum. It won't take but a minute." She came to a breathless halt and nodded at Baxter. "Good to see you again, Mr. Baxter. I hope you are enjoying your stay in Badgers End?"

"Very much so, Mrs. Chubb. Thank you."

Impatiently Cecily interrupted. "What was it you wanted, Mrs. Chubb?"

"Oh, well, mum, it's about Ethel. She wants her old job back again—"

"Yes, yes, I know. Gertie told me. I've already discussed it with my . . . with Mr. Ridlington. He advised me that we could not afford to hire her back."

"Yes, mum, I know. But Gertie had another idea."

Cecily listened while Mrs. Chubb explained Gertie's proposal. When the housekeeper finally finished talking, Cecily nodded. "It sounds like a very good idea."

"Perhaps you could discuss it with Mr. Ridlington, mum?" Mrs. Chubb said hopefully.

"That won't be necessary." Glancing over at Ned, who seemed to be thoroughly confusing the colonel, as usual, Cecily lowered her voice. "As a matter of fact," she murmured, "Mr. Ridlington will be leaving the hotel today."

Mrs. Chubb looked shocked. "Really, mum? I had no idea."

"Yes, well, we'll discuss that later." Cecily sent an urgent glance at the grandfather clock. "Please tell Ethel that I will be most happy to take her back under the new arrangements. In fact, I should be able to give Gertie a raise, which should help matters out with Daisy."

The housekeeper beamed. "Why, thank you, mum. Gertie will be most pleased, I'm sure. Very generous of you, mum. You won't regret it, I'll see to it."

"It will be well worth it, Mrs. Chubb, to have Ethel back in the fold."

She barely waited for the housekeeper to leave before tugging on Baxter's arm. "Come," she whispered fiercely, "before Colonel Fortescue catches sight of us. We haven't another minute to spare."

She assured herself that Baxter was following close behind, then sped up the stairs as fast as she was able. Reaching the first landing, she waited for him to join her.

They were both puffing by the time he stood beside her. "You are in a thundering hurry," he said, glancing behind him. "That old fool would have to have wings on his heels to catch up with us."

"I am not so worried about the colonel as I am the

bishop," Cecily said, still speaking in a low voice. "He is taking afternoon tea in the dining room. It should not be too long before he is finished."

Baxter frowned. "What has the bishop got to do with anything?"

Cecily glanced down the hallway. "It's his suite we will be searching," she whispered.

Baxter stared at her as if she'd gone quite mad.

"Come on." Once more she tugged on his arm. "We have to hurry now. We don't have much time."

Baxter dug in his heels. "The bishop? You want me to search the bishop's suite?"

Cecily gave him an impatient look. "Don't argue, Baxter. We don't have time to debate the issue." Without waiting for his response she hurried down the hallway to the bishop's suite. She had the master key fitted and turned by the time he reached her side.

"Are you aware of the consequences if you are wrong about this?" he muttered. "Surely you can't suspect the bishop of stealing the chalice?"

"Not only stealing it," Cecily said as she opened the door and peered in, "but murdering for it, as well." Finding the room empty, as she'd expected, she walked in. Immediately she saw the glass case with the fake chalice standing on the bureau.

Baxter closed the door softly, saying, "I cannot believe I am assisting you in this bizarre venture. Not only will we suffer dire consequences from the police if you are mistaken, but just imagine the divine retribution we shall endure for violating the privacy of a bishop, no less."

"The trouble with you, Baxter," Cecily murmured, "is your deplorable lack of confidence in my abilities." She headed for the bedroom and opened the door.

He followed her into the room and startled her by coming

up close enough behind her to whisper in her ear. "If I remember, your deductions were somewhat amiss yesterday when you were certain our murderer was Miss Primrose Parsons. You were at that point convinced the murderer was a woman. Much as I am willing to give you the benefit of the doubt, nothing on this good earth will convince me that Bishop John Hornsworth is a woman, much less a murderer."

Standing that close to him, alone together in a private suite, Cecily found it difficult to concentrate on much at all. "Do be quiet, Baxter," she said irritably. "Please do me the favor of searching the bishop's dresser drawers, before he comes back and surprises us both."

"If that should happen, we will both be damned in hell, if you'll pardon me for saying so." Turning away from her, he tugged open the nearest drawer.

Her heart was beating most uncomfortably. She wasn't sure if it was the anxiety of having to prove she was right or the dangerous light she had seen in Baxter's eyes just before he turned away. That he was displeased with her was quite evident. She hoped with all her heart that they would not part at odds with each other. That she could not bear.

"I can see nothing here in the drawers," Baxter said, pulling another one open.

"Did you look underneath the clothes?"

He glanced at her, his expression grim. "There are no clothes in here. The drawers are quite empty."

She made a small sound of distress. "The wardrobe?"

Baxter pulled open the doors. "Also quite empty. The bishop must have already packed his belongings."

"He is expecting to catch the evening train." Cecily looked around the room. Spotting a couple of large travel bags in the corner of the room, she headed for them. "Would you be good enough to search the sitting room for me, Baxter, while I look in these bags?"

"If you'll tell me what I'm looking for."

She looked back at him. "The chalice, of course."

Baxter nodded. "Of course. The bishop stole the Helms-boro chalice, put a fake in its place, killing two men in the process, and is now intending to transport two chalices back to London with him."

"Baxter, please?"

"Oh, very well." He disappeared, and heart thumping, she surveyed the bags. In spite of her confidence in her deductions, she had been known to be wrong before. More than once, in fact. Baxter was right. If she should be wrong this time, the consequences could be quite severe. She could, in fact, be putting her entire business at risk. She could lose the Pennyfoot Hotel.

Taking a deep breath to steady her nerves, she reached for the smaller of the bags. If she were wrong, or if somehow the bishop had outwitted her and she was unable to prove it, she wanted to be alone when she made that discovery.

Her fingers trembled as she unfastened the bag. Inside was an assortment of gentleman's attire, together with a pair of house shoes and various toiletries. A large Bible nestled in the bottom, resting on the magnificent robes the bishop had worn at the ceremony the day before.

Closing the bag, Cecily reached for the second. It was heavier. A good deal heavier. Eagerly now, she opened the clasps. There was a single item in there, wrapped inside a thick, padded smoking jacket.

Carefully Cecily parted the folds of the green velvet fabric. The rich, red glow of rubies flashed in the sunlight from the window, their magnificence rivaled only by the brilliant green fire of emeralds. She held her breath and blinked hard. There, in her hands, lay the Helmsboro chalice.

For a long moment she let the heady rush of relief and triumph overwhelm her, then she called out softly, "Baxter? Look what I've found."

At the same moment, she heard Baxter mutter a loud curse. Then another voice spoke clearly from the other side of the sitting room. "What in the world do you think you are doing, my good man?" demanded the bishop.

Cecily scrambled to her feet as Baxter muttered on a note of desperation, "I wish to God I knew."

CHAPTER

❖ 20 ❖

"Why, Bishop," Cecily exclaimed as she reached the doorway of the sitting room, "how fortunate that you should arrive at this moment. I need you to explain something for me."

Standing by the bureau, one hand still on the opened drawer, Baxter gave her a look that would have made Attila the Hun tremble.

The bishop appeared stunned at the sight of her. Finally finding his voice, he spluttered, "Mrs. Sinclair! I am shocked at this intrusion. I can't imagine why you and this . . . gentleman should invade my room. I demand an explanation at once."

Cecily smiled at Baxter. "I believe you have met Baxter. He used to be my manager."

225

Baxter looked at her as if she had gone completely insane. "This is preposterous, madam," the bishop thundered, his face darkening to a dull red. "I demand to know why you are both skulking in my bedroom."

"Only one of us was skulking in your bedroom," Cecily pointed out.

Baxter made a small sound of despair as the bishop took a threatening step forward. "Mrs. Sinclair, I do not believe you understand the seriousness of this situation."

Abandoning her lighthearted tone, Cecily said quietly, "I understand very well. I confess that we are guilty of invading your privacy. I must ask you, however, to kindly explain how you happen to have two almost identical Helmsboro chalices in your possession."

For a moment it seemed as if the bishop was completely bereft of speech. Out of the corner of her eye, Cecily saw Baxter move closer to her side.

After a moment or two, the bishop said carefully, "I always carry a copy of the chalice with me. The copy is placed on display, in case of theft. The public is none the wiser, and I can keep the genuine chalice safely under lock and key."

Baxter sharply drew in his breath.

Cecily merely smiled. "I must commend you, Bishop. That explanation sounds quite plausible. I might even have believed it, had I not discussed the matter with Mrs. Carter-Holmes and the vicar. They are both quite willing to swear that the case you carried in was a great deal heavier than the case you carried out, suggesting that the chalice had been exchanged for a fake after you put it on display. That might take a little more explaining, I would say."

"I fail to see how the vicar and that ridiculous mother of his could possibly perceive such a thing," the bishop said, beginning to look desperate.

"If I might remind you," Cecily said as Baxter sidled even closer, "the vicar helped you to lift the case upon the pedestal. Both he and Mrs. Carter-Holmes were impressed by the weight of the chalice. During a rehearsal by the dance troupe later in the week, the case was dislodged from its perch. The vicar managed to catch it before it fell. He noticed at once the difference in the weight."

For several long moments the bishop stared at her, seemingly attempting to invent another plausible excuse. Then, like a child seeing a favorite toy snatched away from him, his face crumpled. He staggered over to an armchair and sank down on it, his face buried in his hands. "I should have known the good Lord would not allow me to own what is not mine," he muttered.

Cecily let out her breath. For a bad moment or two she had worried that he might not break down. If he had stubbornly declared his innocence, being a holy man of such prominence, he might well have been given the benefit of the doubt.

Taking a seat on a chair nearby, she said gently, "Perhaps you should tell us what happened."

The bishop shook his head but after a moment began speaking in a voice weak with despair. "I had never coveted anything in my life until I set eyes on the Helmsboro chalice. I am a collector of religious antiques, and the chalice is quite the most remarkable, glorious artifact I have ever seen. I knew the moment I saw it that I had to have it.

"I knew, of course, that even had I been in a position to afford it, which I am not, the church would not sell such a valuable possession. I tried to put such thoughts out of my mind, but I could not. The chalice haunted me day and night, until finally it became an obsession."

Quietly Baxter moved the remaining chair closer to Cecily and sat down.

"So you decided to steal it," Cecily said, feeling a stirring of sympathy for the bishop. Then, remembering Will Jones, she hardened her heart.

"Yes." The bishop dropped his hands and lifted his face to the ceiling. "Heaven help me, I could not seem to fight the obsession. I hired a man to make the exchange for me. I had heard that he was prepared to do almost anything if the price was right. A price I could afford."

"Sid Barker," Cecily said softly.

The bishop nodded. "There just wasn't any other way to own the chalice. I arranged for it to be on display at Saint Bartholomew's. I remembered the vicar was somewhat inept and that the parish was small enough to attract little attention. I had also learned about the feast held this week and that the vicar would be in attendance. It seemed to be the perfect opportunity."

"And it would have been," Cecily said, "had it not been for Will Jones."

"Divine interference, no doubt," the bishop said gloomily. "I received a letter from the vicar, advising me to book a room as early as possible at your hotel because of a large group of bicycle club members who would also be staying here for the festivities. I ordered Mr. Barker to sign on as a member of that club."

"It was my understanding that the club was for women only," Baxter said.

The bishop sighed. "That is correct. Mr. Barker changed his name to that of a fictitious wife, however. Then, at the last minute, he announced that his wife had taken ill and that he was traveling without her.

"We planned the exchange to take place while everyone was at the feast. I was assured that the church remained open until after dark, when the doors were then locked. It was obviously easier to walk in before dark, while the church was empty. Besides, I did not want to take the risk of the vicar seeing a light in the church after dark and raising the alarm."

"But the church wasn't empty," Cecily prompted as the bishop fell silent.

"No," he said with a sigh. "I had forgotten about the bell ringer. He spotted Mr. Barker in the act of exchanging the chalices. Mr. Barker panicked, I'm afraid. He hit him with the only weapon he had. The Helmsboro chalice itself. Unfortunately he didn't take into account the weight of the cup. He assured me he did not intend to kill the man."

"When did he tell you that?" Cecily asked.

"Not until I confronted him several days later. At the time, he was still in a state of panic. He put the body in the trap that he'd borrowed from the hotel and took it up to the cliffs, where he threw the unfortunate man into the sea. It was then he remembered that the bells had not been rung.

"He could not take the chance of someone noticing the fact and investigating the cause, since he had not yet completed the exchange. He then went back to the church, rang the bells himself, then returned to the hotel with the chalice."

Once more the bishop buried his face in his hands. "I had no idea at that point that he had killed that poor man."

"Until I told you that the death of Will Jones had not been an accident," Cecily said, remembering how upset the bishop had been to hear the news.

"Precisely. I was furious, of course. I had never intended for anyone to be hurt. All I wanted was the chalice. I had paid a lot of money to have the copy made. I really didn't think anyone would notice the difference until it was too late to do anything about it. Of course, when I discovered that a man had died because of my obsession, I was beside myself. I confronted Sid Barker with what I had learned."

"He attacked you?" Cecily thought about the delicate-looking man who had died. It would not have been difficult for the bishop to overpower him. Sid Barker could not have been too perceptive if he had expected to escape unhurt.

"Not exactly." Once more the bishop stared up at the ceiling, as if asking forgiveness. "He demanded more money. He said he hadn't bargained on killing someone, and now the price had risen. I threatened to inform the constabulary of what he had done, and he in turn assured me I would hang as an accomplice."

His voice rose, and his hands described wild arcs in the air as he talked. "I was out of my mind with rage and frustration. Everything I had done, the terrible sin I had committed, was all for nothing. That stupid little man had ruined everything. Furious, and without thinking, I struck out at him."

Baxter edged even closer to Cecily, until his chair almost touched hers. Silence fell in the room as the bishop slowly lowered his hands.

"He fell," he said, his voice almost a whisper now. "His head hit the fireplace over there with a terrible crack. He lay still, and I knew he was dead. I didn't know what to do. I felt he deserved to die, although I had not meant to kill him.

"I decided to give him a Christian burial in the churchyard. I waited until dark, took a horse from the stable and led it down to the church with the body across its back. If I had met someone, I would have explained that the man was drunk and I was taking him home."

"So you dug the grave and buried him there," Cecily said, beginning to feel sorry for him again.

"Yes, God rest his soul. I dug in a spot between two other graves, prayed over his body, then covered him with dirt and grass. I hoped that no one would notice until long after I had left the village."

Again he was silent, and Cecily rose. "I must ask you to

wait here with Baxter, Bishop, while I go down to see if the constable has arrived. I sent for him some time ago."

The bishop lifted his face to look at her. "I am ready to face the music now, Mrs. Sinclair. It is almost a relief to have it over. Though I must say, I fear meeting my Maker far more than anything the constabulary can do to me."

"Let us hope it will not come to that," Cecily said quietly. She left him staring into space with Baxter uneasily watching him.

She felt tired now as she made her way down the stairs. Soon she would be facing her own crisis with Baxter. Compared to that, her recent tribulations paled in significance.

It was some time later before Cecily was able to keep her rendezvous with Baxter in the roof garden. P.C. Northcott had arrived and listened to Cecily's brief account of what had happened; after that he took the bishop into custody. For once the constable had managed to leave with his charge without causing a major upheaval.

Now Cecily stood at the wall, looking out across the sea to the misty horizon. Already dusk was gathering, darkening the sky above the smooth line of the ocean. The nights were beginning to draw in. Soon it would be winter again, bringing the cold winds and rain to chill the hotel. Even now, she could sense a faint nip in the air.

"Quite remarkable," Baxter said quietly, a little too close behind her.

She turned her head to glance at him over her shoulder. She had thought he referred to the view, but his gaze was intent upon her face. Unsettled, she asked lightly, "What is it you find so remarkable?"

"Why, your shrewdness, of course. How could you possibly have been so certain that the bishop had stolen the chalice, when you had not the slightest idea of it yesterday?"

Cecily smiled. "I saw him take the case off the pedestal this morning. Since Algie had known right away that the weight of the case had changed, I wondered why the bishop hadn't appeared to notice it. After all, he'd had a great deal more experience with the chalice than had Algie. Yet he made no mention of the discrepancy, suggesting that he already knew the chalice was a fake."

"Ah." Baxter nodded. "Even so, did you really suspect him of murder?"

"Not so much of murder, perhaps, but certainly of being the person who buried Sid Barker." Cecily turned back to gaze across the harbor, where lights were beginning to twinkle in the cottages lining the foot of the cliffs. "You see, I noticed the bishop's shoes. The heels were built up to give him height. I remember, then, that Phoebe had mentioned the bishop seemed taller than when she'd last seen him. Had it not been for that, I might have thought twice about attempting to expose him as the thief."

"I'm happy that your suspicions were justified," Baxter murmured. "I hate to think what penance we would have paid had you falsely accused the bishop of theft and murder. As it is, it would seem that his vanity was his undoing,"

"As often happens," Cecily agreed. "I suppose we were fortunate the bishop chose to confess. He is not, however, an evil man, but a very weak one. I believed him when he said it was a relief to have it over. I don't believe he would have enjoyed the chalice, even if he had managed to avoid being caught with it. His guilt would have become too much to bear."

They stood in companionable silence for a moment or two, then Baxter broke the spell. "I think it is time to change the subject," he abruptly announced.

Cecily curled her fingers into her palms. Now that the

moment she had dreaded was at hand, she prayed she would have the strength to maintain her composure.

She turned to face him, arranging her features into a smile. "I have a feeling that what you are about to say is of great importance."

"Indubitably."

Although his tone was light, she was deeply disturbed to see the signs of strain on his face. Whatever he had to tell her, she knew he would not easily find the words.

"Cecily." He paused, then cleared his throat and stretched his neck in the nervous gesture that was so endearingly familiar. "I should tell you that I left the Pennyfoot Hotel because I had some . . . personal matters to resolve. I could not speak of them at the time, since I wasn't at all certain of my intentions."

Scarcely daring to breathe, she waited for him to continue. After a while, he said hesitantly, "I was having difficulties with our relationship, Cecily."

Her throat constricted, but she merely nodded. "I sensed that was it. I'm sorry, Baxter. I should have been more sensitive—"

"Please!" He held up his hand in a sharp gesture. "Let me finish. I knew that I had a great deal of soul-searching to do, and I needed the time and space to come to terms with my conflicting thoughts. I needed to be alone—without the distractions of the hotel and especially of you."

Where had she gone wrong? she thought dismally. She loved him so much, yet she had hurt him. Unintentionally, perhaps, but nevertheless she had driven him away. She looked up at him, her heart filled with remorse.

"Dear God," Baxter muttered, "please, do not look at me like that. This is none of your doing. It was my rigid adherence to my principles and outdated ideals that were the cause of my turmoil. My desperate need to keep my place was constantly at war with my . . . regard for you. I could not condone my feelings, and I felt trapped by my position. The only way out, as far as I could see, was to put some distance between us, until I had sorted out the confusion in my mind."

She searched his face, trying desperately to understand what he was trying to tell her. When he didn't speak, she said quietly, "And now?"

He lifted his face momentarily to the star-studded sky, then, in a voice strong with resolve, he announced, "I would like to resume my duties at the Pennyfoot, Cecily. I realize now that this is where I belong. I could never be happy living in the city. I miss Badgers End. I miss the hotel, and especially the people who have become my friends."

Her blazing joy was short-lived when he interrupted her exclamation with a quick shake of his head. "Don't be too hasty in accepting my proposition, Cecily. I must warn you that if I stay, things will have to change."

His words hit her like a cold blast of wind. She wanted to plead with him not to change anything. She wanted things the way they were. She wasn't at all sure she could live and work in the Pennyfoot with him without the warmth of his friendship and the hope of something deeper. It would be so terribly difficult to accept the fact that although the man had returned to her, she had lost all hope of his love.

"In what way?" she asked, managing to sound indifferent.

"In every way." Without warning, he reached out and grasped her elbows. "Beginning with this."

To her utter astonishment and heady delight, he bent his head and gently pressed his lips to hers. It was a tender kiss. A kiss full of wary promise. A token of understanding between them. It took her breath away.

He let her go and stood back, his expression so full of apprehension that she almost laughed. "Oh, my," she said, her voice as breathless as if she'd raced up the attic stairs, "you certainly are full of surprises."

"Pleasant ones, I hope?"

Inexplicably, her eyes filled with tears. "Indubitably."

He smiled, a little ruefully. "I was afraid I'd misjudged your feelings for me."

"And I was so certain I was being hideously transparent."

His rich laughter rang out. "You, my dear madam, are the most inscrutable woman I have yet to meet."

"Then we make a good match. I was quite certain you intended to turn your back on all of us."

The affection in his eyes was joyfully plain to read. "I could never do that now."

She lifted an eyebrow at him. "Do you really want your job back? It will mean being my manager again."

"With a difference. Although I shall maintain the proper air of decorum whenever we are together in our respective roles within the hotel, I want you to understand that I no longer consider myself your inferior."

She hurried to reassure him. "Of course not, Baxter. I have never considered you as such."

"Nevertheless, I should like to put the matter on an official footing. I would like to purchase an equal share of the Pennyfoot, thereby making us partners."

If he'd surprised her before, he'd certainly surpassed himself with this latest revelation. She found it impossible to answer him.

"I had a stroke of luck on the stock market, thanks to some shrewd advice from my employer at the bank. It should be enough to buy half of your equity in the hotel."

She nodded, saying weakly, "You do realize, of course, that you are buying property that is deeply in debt? My equity amounts to very little, I'm afraid."

"Which is why I'm able to afford it." He held out his hand to her. "Do we have an agreement?"

She hesitated. "What would you have done if I hadn't fired Malcolm?"

"I knew it was just a matter of time. I had him investigated before I came down to Badgers End. I knew quite well that you would not be able to tolerate him for longer than a week or two."

She should be angry with him, she thought, but who could resist that boyish grin and smug expression? "You think of everything, Mr. Baxter."

"Indeed I do, dear madam. Are we partners?"

She took his hand and clasped it, her heart soaring with joy. "Partners." The memory of his kiss lingered sweetly on her lips. She was going to enjoy this new arrangement.